HOPING FOR HAWTHORNE

TARA GRACE ERICSON

SILVER FOUNTAIN PRESS

Paperback ISBN-13: 978-1-949896-08-4
Ebook ISBN-13: 978-1-949896-09-1

CONTENTS

This book is dedicated to those who have helped me push past my fears and embrace God's plan for me.

You have made them a little lower than the angels
and crowned them with glory and honor.
You made them rulers over the works of your hands;
You put everything under their feet;
all flocks and herds, and the animals of the wild,
the birds in the sky, and the fish in the sea,
all that swim the paths of the seas.

Psalm 8:5-8

*L*aura Bloom stirred honey into her tea and looked absently out the window overlooking the rolling hills of Bloom's Farm. In the fields within her view, neatly planted rows of vegetables had already been harvested. The chilly fall morning was made gloomier by the dense fog lingering in the valleys. It would burn off later in the day, but for now it obstructed her view of the rest of their property.

Her daughter, Poppy was doing a wonderful job with the crops, rapidly growing their organic produce business. Laura's heart warmed at the thought of her seven children—six beautiful girls and one charming young man—each with a special role to play in the success of the family business. Oh, Hawthorne. More than the rest, her son laid heavy on her heart most mornings. Far outnumbered by his sisters, Hawthorne had never been content on the farm. What could she do though, but worry and pray?

Laura clicked her tongue thinking about Hawthorne and his resistance to anything resembling real responsibility. She tried to pin-point when Hawthorne had become this devil-may-care version of the positive and kind-hearted young man she remembered as a teenager. As the second oldest, Hawthorne stepped into the role of protective older brother early on. Then, somewhere along the way, he pushed back against the mantle of responsibility.

Hawthorne lived at the old house with his sister, Daisy, and kept himself busy during the days with whatever odd projects needed done around the property, never sitting still long enough to dwell on his own discontentedness. But Laura knew how he spent his evenings. What Hawthorne needed wasn't a career or even a girlfriend. Hawthorne needed to realize the thing holding him back in life was himself and his so-called friends. Again, Laura lifted a prayer to God for Hawthorne's faith to be strengthened.

Perhaps the right woman was exactly what Hawthorne needed to shake him from his routine. It couldn't hurt to pray for his future wife, just as she had since he was born. Maybe God would give an answer this time.

1

-----

*H*awthorne shifted on his barstool, sipping his drink as his friend, Shayne, recounted a raucous story Hawthorne had heard a dozen times before. He resisted the urge to sigh. This was the third night this week they'd spent doing the same thing. There wasn't much to do in Terre Haute, Indiana, but it was better than staying at the farm where he lived with his parents and sisters.

He pulled himself back into the conversation, ribbing Shayne on his over-embellished narrative about waiting too long for a date to be ready. "It was five minutes, not thirty. Don't be such a drama queen."

Shayne waved a hand, "Whatever. Either way, it

took forever, and if I hadn't thought I'd get lucky after dinner, I never would have waited."

Roars of laughter erupted from the group of men before Craig chimed in with his own online dating experience.

Eager to feel less disconnected, Hawthorne followed it with a story of his own. Since dating apps never held his interest, it was one of the few he had.

As he described his date, doing some embellishing of his own, his friends jeered and cracked up. Hawthorne ignored the twinge of conscience and delivered his last joke with gusto. Holding up two fingers, he made eye contact with his enraptured listeners. "Two words, fellas. Woof, woof." Howls of laughter rang out and the short, curvy waitress ducked between Shayne and Hawthorne, grabbing empty glasses and delivering chips and salsa.

Shayne flirted shamelessly with the waitress, rubbing a hand down her arm with a wink. "Thank you, sweetheart. Now, make sure you walk away nice and slow so we can enjoy the view."

With a shake of his head, Hawthorne laughed at his friend's antics. Sure, sometimes Shayne got carried away, but he was a nice guy for the most part. The waitress ducked out of reach and gave a tight-lipped smile. "Can I get you guys anything else?"

"What are you offering?" Shayne asked with a leer.

"I can think of a few things I'd like," Craig added to Shayne's suggestive proposition.

Wendy tensed and looked toward the bartender. When she opened her mouth, Hawthorne was surprised to hear a strong, feminine voice coming from behind him instead.

"Leave the woman alone, jerks. Can't you just let her do her job without harassing her?" The venom in the voice practically stung as it continued loudly above the music. "Believe it or not, not every girl wants you and your immature, demeaning views on women."

Shayne's mouth gaped and Hawthorne raised his eyebrows. Who did this girl think she was?

He turned around to look at her and saw a beautiful woman with a fierce, angry look. Momentarily, her eyes widened and her mouth dropped open, surprise crossing her features. Hawthorne racked his brain; did he know her? She looked familiar, but Hawthorne wasn't sure from where. Maybe he'd seen her here before. Was she on the dating app he'd downloaded and swiped through? Her gray eyes narrowed at him, flashing with irritation again. A colorful headband contrasted starkly with the pale, golden strands of her hair, tied back in a loose pony-tail. *Stunning.*

Shayne was still sputtering his objections to the interruption. Wendy slipped away in the midst of the distraction and went to take care of her other tables.

"Hawthorne Bloom, your mama raised you better than this." Hawthorne's mouth dropped open. She knew his name? This girl was beautiful, why didn't he remember her?

"Look, lady. Mind your own-"

Hawthorne interrupted Craig and turned fully in his chair. "Do I know you?" The woman leaned back in her chair and crossed her arms.

"I guess not," she replied with a raised eyebrow. Then, leaving cash for her check, she grabbed her book and jacket and walked away from the table where she'd been sitting alone. After two steps, she turned back. "Your waitress is a person. Leave her alone or treat her with respect. All of you," she waved a hand at the table of wide-eyed guys, "grow up. And you?" she pointed at Hawthorne, "Find some new friends. I would have thought you were better than this."

With that parting shot, she weaved through tables and ducked around patrons of the bar.

Shayne jabbered about disrespect and how it was all innocent fun. But Hawthorne sat, frozen on his chair and staring at the path the stranger had taken on her way out. But she wasn't a stranger. Or was she? Somehow, she knew him, and he couldn't shake the nagging feeling that he recognized her.

Swallowing the urge to chase after her, Hawthorne turned back to his friends and jumped into the conversation with a shake of his head. "That was weird."

"Yeah, man. Did you know her?" someone asked from across the table.

With a baffled shrug he said, "No. Not that I can remember," still racking his brain for a name that wouldn't come.

With that, Craig was off on a story of the time he ran into a one-night stand he didn't remember at all. Hawthorne laughed at the appropriate places, but his mind was on the gutsy blonde with familiar eyes. She'd been disappointed in him. Join the club, beautiful. It seemed someone was always disappointed in him at home. Why should it bother him now? He hadn't been the one flirting with the waitress. And even if he thought Shayne and Craig took it too far, Wendy was a good sport. They were just having a little fun. His eyes fell closed and he tipped his head back at the ceiling when he realized what he had been saying before Shayne came on to Wendy.

Woof, woof. He winced at the thought of the woman overhearing the crude comment.

No wonder she thought he was scummy. Why did it matter, though? He didn't know her. Still, she seemed to know him or, at least, his family, and her reaction rankled. He didn't want to be a bad guy. Even before the mystery woman's interruption, Hawthorne couldn't help but feel like this same old routine was nothing but emptiness parading as a life.

At least he wasn't living in his parents' basement anymore; he'd moved into the old farmhouse with Daisy about eight months ago as they worked to fix it up. Daisy was determined to turn the old homestead into a bed and breakfast and while Hawthorne wasn't a contractor by any means, he was pretty handy and could help with smaller projects as he had time. It was still on the farm, though. Not exactly far from the nest.

Days at the farms. Nights at the bar. Saturday morning brunch at the main house.

Despite the loud country music and crowd of people at the bar, Hawthorne felt isolated. Even the constant presence of his family and the dozen other staff members at the farm couldn't chase away the sense of loneliness.

He'd been friends with Shayne and Craig since high school, screwing around during shop class and sneaking chewing tobacco behind the bleachers at the football stadium. And after things with his company went south, they welcomed him back into the fold.

No expectations. No judgment.

He kept ignoring the feeling, but for the past six months, he found himself annoyed by the constant stream of short-term relationships and the same shallow conversations about nothing but girls, cars and weightlifting. Hawthorne dated, a week or two here and there, but nothing like his friends who had every dating and hook-up app on the market. They spent more time primping in the morning than any of Hawthorne's six sisters.

If he didn't have his friends, though, who did he have? Hawthorne loved his family and each of his sisters, especially. But there was only so much sisterly love a guy could take; six sisters meant an awful lot of estrogen. His parents were wonderful, but his dad was determined that his one-and-only son should take over the family business.

It was too much pressure.

Hawthorne enjoyed his current role as the wandering handyman. Whatever needed attention, he took care of it. No expectations. No drastic consequences. Then, at the end of the day, he could leave and have a good time with his buddies.

Work to live, not live to work.

His sisters all had such concrete goals. Daisy cared far too much about her bed and breakfast, as evidenced by the minor breakdown she'd had this morning when the lumberyard said the tiles she ordered wouldn't be in for two more weeks. Rose practically slept with her precious goats and Poppy was growing the organic produce business every season. When he thought of them, Hawthorne filled with pride at the accomplishments of his sisters, but it was tinged with envy. It was easy to feel aimless surrounded by a family so focused on purpose and so trusting in God's plan.

He just wanted to have a good time, and it didn't seem like such a bad goal to have. However, with the last swallow of his watered-down drink, Hawthorne considered whether these nights with his friends could really count as such. If he was honest, the best part of the evening was the unexpected conversation with the fiery stranger. Hawthorne glanced toward the door again, hoping she'd walk back through it.

He'd probably never see her again, and he wasn't sure exactly why that thought bothered him so much.

AVERY CHASE WAS VIBRATING. Confronting the obnoxious guys at the bar had been nearly instinctual. After years in a male-dominated workplace, she wasn't afraid to hold her own—or come to the rescue of someone who thought they couldn't speak up themselves.

When Hawthorne Bloom turned around, Avery had about dropped the drink in her hand. Thankfully, he hadn't recognized her. It had been over fifteen years, but her heart still jumped out of her chest in response to his presence. Careful to park straight, Avery pulled in front of her apartment building and grabbed her bag from the backseat.

Avery moved away from western Indiana with her parents fifteen years ago, heartbroken and convinced she would never return. By the time she was old enough, it seemed there was no point. All her friends had lost touch, including the friends she spent summers with at Bloom's farm. And their out-of-her-league older brother, Hawthorne.

Avery dropped her canvas shoulder bag on the floor next to the small, secondhand sofa and collapsed into the floral cushion with a groan. Hawthorne Bloom had been her best friends' brother. Their cute and athletic, slightly older brother. While Avery spent time at the unofficial Bloom's Farm Summer Camp with Daisy and Poppy, Hawthorne was always there making her increasingly aware of her clumsy and awkward fourteen-year-old self.

Back then, he'd at least known her name, unlike tonight. It was an especially timely ego check, as she celebrated her own success, to realize the boy she'd always considered her "one who got away" didn't even remember her. Perhaps even worse, she frowned, somewhere along the line he apparently turned into a jerk. With parents like Laura and Keith, how had Hawthorne ended up running in a circle of overgrown fraternity stereotypes?

It had been a bad idea to stop by the bar, but she'd wanted to celebrate. Her grant proposal had been accepted, and she would be working on a new sustainable battery technology with Dr. Elliot. That's why she'd chosen academia—the chance to use her engineering degree to uncover something ground-breaking.

Avery opened her eyes to stare at the ceiling before glancing around her small apartment. For the first time, she had her own place and was slowly forging her path in academic circles, creating a solid reputation as a researcher and teaching professor. Foolishly, Avery had been hopeful God brought her here to reconnect with Hawthorne. Her embarrassingly thorough social media stalking of her old friends hadn't revealed any weddings in the Bloom family.

After tonight though, it couldn't be clearer that Hawthorne wasn't the guy for her. Avery had traveled that road early in college and she wouldn't be fooled by the carefree, impulsive attitude again. Avoiding Bloom's Farm would be simple, and avoiding Hawthorne couldn't be that hard in a town the size of Terre Haute. Two days later, though, Avery discovered it wouldn't be quite as easy as she'd hoped.

2

"*A*very Chase, is that you?"

Avery looked up from the handwritten grocery list in her hand and found the source of the overly loud question. The familiar face of Laura Bloom walked toward her down the pasta aisle, pushing her own grocery cart. Avery couldn't help but smile at the aged version of the woman who had been like a second mother to her. Until she was fourteen, Avery spent days during the summer at the farm while her own parents worked. Those days had been filled with hard work, endless exploration, and troublemaking. Then Avery moved to Colorado and had to say good-bye.

Avery tried to focus on the woman standing in

front of her, instead of the thoughts of Hawthorne brought to the surface. "Hello Miss Laura," Avery replied cheerfully. It wasn't Laura's fault her son was a Grade A buffoon.

"I didn't know you were back in the area! Are your parents back as well? It would be so good to see them again."

Avery gave a small smile and shook her head. "No, they are still out in Freedom, Colorado. I don't think anything could get them to leave."

Laura gave a nod of understanding. "I'm sure it is beautiful. We were certainly sorry to see them leave; they were some of our closest friends back then. Goodness, what has it been? Ten years?"

"Nearly fifteen now, actually."

"Wow. Time flies! What brings you back?"

Avery straightened. "I got a new job at the University. I'm teaching and doing research in the chemical engineering department."

Laura grinned broadly in response. "I'm not at all surprised, Avery. You were always so smart and such a hard worker. Congratulations!"

Avery filled with pride. It had always mattered to her what the Bloom family thought of her. She'd always wished she could be a part of it. While Daisy always joked that Laura and Keith would just adopt her, Avery had spent countless birthday wishes on marrying into the family. Unfortunately, with six girls and one boy, her odds were low—and they dropped all the way to non-existent after the other night.

"Thank you. It's nice to be back."

Laura stepped around her cart and opened her arms to wrap Avery in a hug. "Oh, you just have to come to the farm next week."

Avery shook her head. "You don't have to—"

Laura waved a hand and studied Avery with big, dark, eyes. "Nonsense. The girls will be thrilled to see you. Do any of them know you are back?"

Avery gave a guilty shake of her head. "It's been kind of crazy getting settled in." What Avery didn't say was how scared she was to try to rekindle those old friendships. Thirteen years was a long time to bridge. Hawthorne's personality transplant was evidence of that. What if Daisy and Poppy were horrible? Or, what if she was so different, they no longer had anything in common? Avery hadn't come back to Terre Haute to recapture her friendships; she'd come back for the opportunity at the university. Anything else seemed like asking for too much.

"I'm sure it has, sweetie. But I insist. Everyone will be thrilled to have you visit occasionally. I know I would!" Laura gave Avery's arm a gentle squeeze. "It can't be easy to be so far away from your family. Why don't you come over next Saturday for brunch?"

Brunch sounded harmless; what could go wrong over pancakes? Finally, with a shrug, Avery responded, "Brunch sounds great, Miss Laura."

HAWTHORNE HELD the fence board up with a knee and hammered in two nails. This stupid fence was the bane of his existence. But Rose would probably cry if one of her precious goats ran off again, and he hated it when his sisters cried. Even when it wasn't his fault, it made him feel guilty. His sisters, of course, had capitalized on that weakness repeatedly over the years.

The week had passed with all the hurry of a lame turtle. Instead of his usual evening outings, he'd begged off and wallowed at home. Since the woman at the bar, he couldn't bring himself to spend another evening with his friends. Considering his options, Hawthorne tugged his phone out of his jeans and thumbed through his contacts until he saw Josh's name.

Hey man. It's been awhile. You free tonight?

Josh's reply came quickly.

Good to hear from you! I've got a portrait session at five, but I'd be free around 6:30. Want to hit the bistro?

Sounds good. I'll meet you there.

His mood brightened at the plans for the evening. Josh had been his friend for twenty years, and even though they didn't see each other much anymore, Josh was likely to be better company than any of his friends from college.

That evening, Hawthorne opened the door to the bistro and surveyed the space, admiring the completed renovations. He'd heard nothing but rave reviews since Chrissy hired a chef from Chicago who could apparently turn an ordinary sandwich into something that would knock your socks off. Chrissy was a couple years younger and was close friends with Josh's younger sister, Mandy.

Chrissy greeted him with a smile. "Hey, stranger. Long time no see."

"The place looks great, Chrissy."

Hawthorne grabbed a table along the wall and

waited for his friend. A flash of black leather caught his eye through the front window, and he couldn't help but smile. Josh was an eclectic mix of biker and artist; covered with tattoos Hawthorne could never imagine having. Somehow, it worked for Josh, though. He slipped through the door and scanned the room before spotting Hawthorne against the wall.

Hawthorne stood and extended his hand to his friend, who pulled him into a hug. A few slaps on the back from each of them and they parted.

Slipping off his jacket, Hawthorne spotted several new tattoos on Josh's arms. "Is there even any ink left at the tattoo parlor?"

"Probably just enough for you to get that heart with my name in it you've been wanting," Josh joked as they sat down. "Wow, it's been a minute, hasn't it? What's new in your world?" he asked.

"Not much, man. Same old stuff around the farm, you know how it is."

Josh shook his head. "E-I-E-I-O? Picking goats and riding carrots isn't really my thing," he joked. "I'm glad somebody does it though," he said with a grin. "Actually, I am shooting Chrissy and Todd's wedding there in a few weeks."

"Oh, nice. Lily's done a good job with the event

barn. She's booked almost every weekend," Hawthorne said proudly.

Instead of asking more about the event venue like Hawthorne thought he would, Josh gave a noncommittal hum and changed the subject. "Mandy said Daisy's fixing up the old homestead?"

Hawthorne chuckled. "Yeah, I'm not sure she realized what she was biting off. Mom and Dad invested in it, but I think her budget is about maxed out. She was in a heated discussion with the contractor before I left." He shook his head at his sister's antics. "She's passionate, which is cool. But she's also... Daisy." He didn't know how to explain it, but he knew Josh would understand. Daisy had always been a whirlwind of activity and ideas, all wrapped up in one over-caffeinated package.

Josh laughed. "That makes sense. Cool for her, though. That's a big project."

After they ordered their dinner, Josh pushed him for answers. "What's going on, man? I don't think we've hung out since that birthday party. What was that, two years ago, now?"

With a sigh, Hawthorne ran a hand through his hair. "I know, I'm sorry I kind of disappeared on you. I envy you, you know?" At Josh's confused look, he continued. "You've got your thing. Your photography, your motorcycle," He gestured to his friend's tattoo-covered arms, "your body-as-a-canvas thing. You've got good friends and, I don't know, it just seems like I don't have any of that."

Josh raised an eyebrow at him. "What do you have?"

"That's the problem. I'm Mr. Fix-it around the farm, which I actually do like. It keeps me busy and I get a paycheck. And I've got my friends, but Shayne and Craig..." Hawthorne hesitated. Josh had met his friends and didn't approve. Which is one of the reasons they hadn't seen each other in so long.

"Shayne and Craig what?" Josh wasn't going to drop it.

"They just... Well, the other night, they were flirting with the waitress and being kind of over-the-top." Hawthorne didn't miss the wrinkle in Josh's brow. "It wasn't a big deal, nothing obnoxious," he tried to defend his friends, but the memory of the beautiful stranger's face appeared in his mind. "Okay, maybe a little obnoxious. Actually, this girl from the other table called them out on it."

"You go, girl," Josh muttered under his breath.

Hawthorne couldn't help but share the rest. "The strangest part was that she knew me. Like, she knew my full name and she acted so disappointed in me."

Josh narrowed his eyes. "And you didn't know her?"

Holding up his hands in surrender, Hawthorne replied, "Nope. She looked familiar, but I could not place her for the life of me. It was so weird."

Josh gave him a skeptical look. "Was she someone you met on a night you might not remember?"

"What? No!" he said firmly. "Look, I know I might not be a saint, but I've never been like Craig and Shayne. Probably too many dang sisters."

Josh smiled, "Probably. But if it had been one of your sisters and people were treating her like Craig and Shayne did?" Josh gave him a questioning glance, pointing out his own hypocrisy.

Hawthorne's jaw clenched, his protective instinct flaring at the hypothetical situation. One thing he always liked about Josh was his no-nonsense attitude about things. "I get your drift. I would never let someone treat my sisters like that."

The food arrived and conversation shifted to lighter topics, but after the food was gone, Josh circled back to what was still on Hawthorne's mind. "What are you going to do?"

"What do you mean?"

"I mean about this girl. Clearly she made an impression, or you wouldn't be talking about her four days later. Do you think you can find her?" Josh asked.

Hawthorne held up his hands in surrender and shook his head. "No way, man. You should have seen the way she looked at me. Like I was manure on the bottom of her boot. I don't know how she knows me, but I'll never see her again anyway."

"If you say so, H. But I wouldn't bet on it." Josh smirked. "Women who tie us up in knots have a habit of never really disappearing."

Seeing a chance to divert attention away from himself, Hawthorne jumped on the comment, "Oh? Just who exactly is tying you up in knots?" Josh had never mentioned a girlfriend in the entire time they'd known each other. Nearly twenty years with no relationships to speak of made a guy wonder. Hawthorne studied Josh's eyes closely.

Josh cleared his throat. "Don't worry about me. You just worry about making sure the next time you see this mysterious stranger, you are proud of how she sees you. I think that has more to do with it than anything. If you aren't proud of who you are, it's easy to be defensive when someone else says something that hits a nerve."

Hawthorne let Josh deflect the question about his own love life, but after a silent moment he followed up. "Do you think she was right about me?"

"The question isn't whether I think she was right. The real question is whether or not you do."

3

*H*awthorne and Daisy stepped down from his truck and walked across the driveway to the front door of the main house. They still lived at the farm, but it was almost a full mile from the old homestead to the main house, and on a chilly Saturday morning, it was worth driving instead of hoofing it.

Opening the door, Hawthorne waved Daisy in ahead of him. The smell of bacon and cinnamon wafted through the air and enveloped him while visions of cinnamon rolls made his mouth start to water. Saturday morning brunch had been a Bloom family tradition ever since Hawthorne could remember. Some of his earliest memories were getting up to help his dad with the animals and coming back to the house for warm plates of bacon, eggs, and pancakes. As they all got older and weeknight dinners were replaced with dance classes, softball, or baseball, Saturday mornings became the one time a week the whole family was guaranteed to be around.

When he and Daisy walked into the open-concept dining room and kitchen, his mom was spreading icing on a full sheet tray of giant cinnamon rolls. Swiping icing from the corner of the pan with his finger, he gave his mom a grateful smile.

His mom tipped her butter knife at him and gave him a pointed look. "Knock it off, Hawthorne Philip."

He gave her a sheepish smile in return, "Is there coffee?"

Laura gestured to the pot behind her. "Should be done by now."

Daisy walked to the refrigerator and dug around until she found the Diet Dr. Pepper she kept stashed in the back of the bottom drawer. "Ah-hah!"

Hawthorne gave her a disgusted look. "Isn't it too early for that?"

Daisy twirled to a seat at the bar, "Never!" She tucked one foot up onto the bar stool where she was perched and rested her soda on her legging-clad thigh.

Poppy wandered in, still wrapping a ponytail holder onto the end of a braid.

"Good morning, sweetheart," Laura said.

"Where's Dad?" Poppy looked around for him.

"I think he just got out of the shower," Laura replied with a glance toward their bedroom door.

Lavender walked through the laundry room and into the kitchen, carrying a jug of orange juice from the refrigerator in the garage. "Oh, hey guys!" She set it on the table and then grabbed a stack of plates from the cupboard by the sink.

Laura spoke up, "We've got an extra this morning, Lovey. Could you set the table for eight?"

Eyebrows rose around the kitchen, but Hawthorne was the first to speak. "Who's coming? Is Andi back in town?" he asked, referring to their sister stationed in Afghanistan with the Army.

"I wish," his mother said kindly. "No, actually I ran into an old friend at the grocery store and invited her to join us. Do you all remember Avery Chase?"

"Avery Chase?" Hawthorne repeated slowly, testing the name and trying to place it.

Daisy straightened, "Oh my goodness, Avery is back?" Daisy's eyes shone with excitement. Avery must be another one of his sisters' friends.

Lavender grabbed another plate and began to set

the table while Poppy and Daisy chattered about memories of Avery. Hawthorne sipped his coffee and gathered from the ongoing prattle that Avery had moved away when Daisy was seventeen, which meant Hawthorne would have been twenty-one. At that age he was hardly concerned with his younger sisters' friends. It was still interesting that his mom had invited the young woman over for brunch, since brunch was typically reserved for family. Maybe this Avery had been closer to his sisters than he realized.

Rose walked in from the laundry room and pulled off her boots. "Good morning, everybody."

Greetings for their youngest sister filled the kitchen as she made her way toward the living room. "I'm going to change my shirt real quick before breakfast. One of the dogs rolled in something before he decided I needed a hug." Rose seemed unbothered, but Hawthorne could smell the foul odor as she passed him.

"I don't smell anything other than your usual delightful scent, sis," he teased. Rose rolled her eyes and gave him a sharp tap on the back of the head before dancing away toward the bedrooms when he tried to retaliate.

Lavender gave an exaggerated gag. "Gross. I'm so glad I don't have to help with animals anymore."

Despite growing up on the farm, Lavender was the least "country" girl Hawthorne had ever met. She adored fashion and spent far too much time online, but Lavender had carved out a nice little niche by managing the farm's social media and website, which was growing more and more important for business. With Daisy's added Bed and Breakfast, it would take on a life of its own.

Just then, a knock on the front door sounded. Daisy jumped up and exclaimed, "I'll get it!" before jogging to the door. Hawthorne heard her squeals and the soft thumps as Daisy jumped on the tile in her socks. He shook his head and took a deep swig of the coffee, finally at a drinkable temperature, as Daisy turned the corner. A familiar flash of blonde hair and an emerald green headband registered with a coffee-filled gasp caught in his throat. Hawthorne felt a stab of pain as he forced himself to swallow and the coughing began.

AVERY FOLLOWED Daisy through the living room and turned the corner to the expansive kitchen. Immediately, her eyes landed on Hawthorne, his coffee cup to his lips. Their eyes met for a split second before he began to cough and sputter and Avery, panicked at the sight of him, turned her gaze to friendlier faces.

Laura cracked eggs into a mixing bowl. "Oh Avery, I'm so glad you're here!" She glanced at her son with concern. "Are you okay, Hawthorne?"

He waved a hand, still coughing. Then, he walked past Avery and into the other room, the noise of his coughing fit dampened by the walls between them.

Poppy came up and gave Avery a quick hug. "It's so good to see you, Avery! It's been so long."

"It really has," Avery replied.

"Can I get you a cup of coffee or hot chocolate?"

"Or a Diet Dr. Pepper?" Daisy grinned, holding up her can of soda.

Avery couldn't help but chuckle at her long-time friend. "Coffee would be wonderful, thank you," she said to Poppy. To Daisy she said, "When did you make the switch to diet?"

Daisy rolled her eyes, "Ugh. Don't remind me. The freshman fifteen finally caught me during senior year and I gave up regular soda after I graduated. When I had to stop dancing, it was a lot harder to burn those extra calories."

Poppy handed Avery a warm mug and Avery

inhaled the rich aroma of fresh coffee. This was worlds better than the coffee in the professors' lounge.

Avery shifted her weight uncomfortably for a moment, but the silence didn't last long. A young woman came into the kitchen and Avery wondered which sister it was. It was hard enough to keep track back when she saw them every day.

"Rose, did you see your father?" Laura asked, answering Avery's question. Avery tried to remember Rose from before she moved, but Rose had only been eleven or twelve. Now, she was a grown woman. It really had been a long time.

Mr. Bloom entered the kitchen with the loud voice Avery remembered fondly. "Good morning, family! Surely, this is the day the Lord has made!" Avery smiled at his exuberance. "And good morning, Avery. Laura told me she invited you; what a wonderful surprise."

Keith kissed his wife on the cheek and swiped some frosting from the edge of a sheet tray filled with cinnamon rolls the size of Avery's face. Laura blushed at his affection, and half-heartedly swatted at his hand.

"Are we all ready to eat?" she asked, handing her husband a plate piled with bacon.

Lavender spoke up, "Looks like we are just waiting on Lily and Hawthorne."

Laura looked toward the living room, "Go make sure he didn't cough up a lung and tell him to get in here or I'm giving his cinnamon roll to Apollo." She set the skillet of scrambled eggs on a trivet on the table, along with the sheet pan of giant cinnamon rolls.

"Apollo?" Avery asked Daisy quietly as Lavender went to find her brother.

They made their way to the table as Daisy explained. "Mom's dog. When Titan died, Mom swore she'd never get another dog. But about six months later, Apollo showed up on the farm. He's the most spoiled dog you've ever seen," she said with obvious affection for her mother.

They settled at the table and Lavender came back in with Hawthorne. Avery watched him, but he never looked in her direction. Lily rushed in behind them, a thick notebook under her arm, apologizing for her tardiness. Hawthorne focused all his attention toward Keith who was about to pray. Keith held out his hands and slowly, each member of the family joined hands in a complete circle. Daisy squeezed Avery's left hand and Poppy held her right, filling her with the familiar sense of belonging she'd always felt with the Bloom family.

Keith began to pray, filling the dining room with his warm, confident tone. "Father God, thank you for this beautiful morning. There is nothing I value more than the family you've blessed me with. We ask your continued hand over Dandelion, stationed overseas. Protect her and bring her home to us safely. Thank you for bringing Avery here this morning, and thank you for this food and the continued blessing of our home and farm. We love you. In Jesus' name, Amen."

A chorus of 'amens' echoed around the table and a flurry of activity erupted as people reached for fruit, bacon, or orange juice. It was worlds different from the family dinners she'd shared over the years with her parents and single sister, Brielle. Brie was four years younger and couldn't be more different from Avery. She still lived in Colorado, happy to live in the small tourist town and work at the mountain resort and ski lodge. Avery's parents were serious and studious, and family dinners at the Chase household felt more like moderated discussions on current events or scientific trivia.

Amidst the sudden chatter, Avery looked across the table, trying to catch Hawthorne's eyes, but he was caught in conversation with Rose two seats down. Was he avoiding her on purpose? Of course he was; she'd humiliated him at the bar in front of his friends. Avery shifted in her seat and sat up straight, absolving herself of the twinge of guilt. Hawthorne was the one hanging out with those lowlife womanizers. She shouldn't feel guilty about what happened; he should.

Laura waved to get Avery's attention across the table and raised her voice above the other conversations. "So, Avery, tell us everything about where you've been the last thirteen years! You mentioned research at the university brought you back to the area?"

Avery was happy to engage and talked about her degree in chemical engineering. Hawthorne's eyes burned her skin as she felt him watching, but this time she refused to acknowledge him. Payback was fair play. Instead, she talked to everyone else, looking around the table without meeting Hawthorne's chocolate-brown eyes. Somehow, Avery knew if she looked at him, it would spiral into a confrontation, and she didn't want to ruin everyone's breakfast. An argument with Hawthorne could wait until she'd had at least two cups of coffee.

4

*H*awthorne tried to listen to Avery relay the last thirteen years of her life as an uninterested party. After all, she was simply his sisters' friend from over a decade ago; but as he listened, he was captivated. Avery laughed and answered questions about why she chose engineering and joked about stodgy old professors who underestimated her because she was blonde.

Why didn't he remember her more from when they were younger? The stroll his family took down memory lane revealed she had been around for five or so years before her family moved. He would have been sixteen the first summer she stayed at the farm. Maybe it was just because she was just a kid back then, but she definitely wasn't a child anymore.

His mother's homemade cinnamon rolls were one of his favorite treats, but this morning he barely tasted his. Distracted by the confident woman sitting directly across the table, Hawthorne choked down his breakfast and tried to leave. "Thanks for breakfast, Mom."

"Don't leave quite yet, honey. We have some family business to cover."

He frowned. Family business? With Avery at the table?

"Nothing serious, Hawthorne." His father waved away his son's unspoken concerns. "We are so proud of all of you. Today, we wanted to celebrate Lily's success with the event business. I never dreamed our little farm would grow as much as it has. It has officially been one year since Lily started renting out the refinished barn." His mom clapped her hands together quietly, and before long, the entire Bloom family was clapping and cheering. Hawthorne let out a whistle.

Lily blushed at the attention. "Thanks, Dad. It's been an adventure. But, if you remember, we do have a wedding there this evening, so I need to get back as soon as possible." She tapped the planner she carried everywhere.

Hawthorne spoke up. "Do you need anything from me today?"

"I don't think so. But I'll text you if I do, okay?"

Lily looked back at their father. "Anything else we need to cover?"

Keith shook his head. "Nope, that's all, Lilypad."

"Great work this year, sweetie," their mother added.

"We are very excited for the opportunities you have all explored for the farm." He looked from sibling to sibling, addressing each in turn.

"Daisy, your bed and breakfast will be a great addition. Poppy, your vineyard and winery are already so beautiful. Lavender, when I see the Bloom's Farm Facebook page, I'm amazed at how you connect with people virtually. Since you started promoting online, our orchard events and produce subscriptions have grown tenfold. Rose, I can't thank you enough for helping me so much with the animals. And Hawthorne," he continued, "this place would probably fall apart without you keeping it all together."

Hawthorne felt his cheeks burn in shame. His contribution to the farm wasn't near as critical as his father made it sound. Especially when compared to his sisters'. But isn't that what he wanted? Too much responsibility was a surefire way to let someone down. He'd learned that lesson once before.

AVERY LISTENED to the impromptu speech with admiration and a bit of jealousy. Her parents had never validated her efforts quite so plainly. Keith and Laura had always been generous with affection and praise, even to her, but she'd forgotten how generous. The changes at Bloom's farm were startling. When she was here as a child, it had seemed an over-whelming operation with crops and animals. But now? It was becoming so much more than that.

What had Keith said about Daisy? A bed and breakfast? That was incredible. She remembered the old homestead; they'd played in the rundown house as young girls, dreaming of their husbands and fami-lies. Heat filled her cheeks as she remembered one particular trait of her "pretend" family—Hawthorne had always been her husband. She'd called him Harry so Daisy wouldn't know, which seemed laugh-able now.

Keith spoke kindly enough about Hawthorne's contribution on the farm, but that didn't mean anything. He was still the man she'd seen in the bar last week. Hawthorne was thirty-three years old, for crying out loud. Shouldn't he be more than a handyman? He'd been in college when she moved away. She racked her brain trying to remember what he'd studied. Had it been business? Or something to do with computers? Whatever it was, clearly it hadn't panned out.

Avery had to let go of this dream she'd carried around for over a decade about the man across the table. He was just like Brandon. Whenever it was time for her to date someone again, he would be completely solid. Was it too much to want someone responsible and committed? Maybe she should say yes to Edward from the chemistry department if he asked her out again. He was nice enough. A bit boring, perhaps. But boring is good. Boring meant responsible and stable, and that was what she wanted.

After brunch wrapped up, Daisy offered Avery a tour of the bed and breakfast. They chatted while Avery drove them to the old house and parked in front. "Wow, Daze! This looks incredible."

Avery must have passed this on the way to the main house without evening noticing all the work that had already been done. The front porch had been completed, and the house was freshly painted.

Cute Adirondack chairs were set on the porch to create a little seating area.

Daisy beamed with pride. "Thank you! There was just something about getting the exterior done that made it feel more attainable. The inside is essentially a warzone," Daisy joked.

Once Avery walked through the front door, she had to agree. Then again, Avery recalled what the house looked like more than ten years ago, and she could see how it was coming together. "Didn't there used to be a wall here?"

Daisy laughed. "Good memory! This used to be the front parlor. And then this was the living room. But I wanted it to be one big space instead. Greg, my contractor, was able to install a beam and take out the wall."

"Wow, that's awesome." Avery treaded carefully across the room, staying on the white paper covered in dusty footprints. "Floors?"

"Mostly original, with a few patches, as long as I can convince Lance to teach me how to patch them."

Avery raised an eyebrow. "Lance?"

Daisy let out a growl. "Lance is Greg's son. And apparently Greg has to get his knee replaced. Which means his ongoing projects are being managed by his far-more-infuriating son and business partner. He was here for the first time the other day." Daisy took a deep breath, and Avery could see her trying to push down the agitation. Daisy had always worn her emotions on her sleeve.

Daisy exhaled and turned to the kitchen. "Anyway, I don't want to talk about Lance." She said his name like a curse word. "Come look at the kitchen. It's coming along."

Avery followed her but made a mental note to follow back up in a few weeks to see how things were going with Lance. It wasn't uncommon for Daisy to be overly dramatic, but it always made for a few good stories.

They stepped into the kitchen and Avery looked around. The minuscule kitchen seemed three times the size she remembered. Daisy led her through a wide opening into a room with a bay window overlooking the valley. "This is the dining room."

"How many rooms do you have?" Avery tried to remember the layout of the second floor.

"There are five bedrooms upstairs. I'll steal one of them to create attached bathrooms for two of the rooms." As they walked up the stairs, Avery trailed a hand up the wooden banister. It had been replaced, or at least sanded and re-stained and was a stark, shining contrast to the chaos of the rest of the space.

They wandered around the upper floor. The bedrooms were small, but should fit queen beds easily. A quick peek in the hallway bathroom revealed floor-to-ceiling baby blue tile and a matching bathtub peeked out from behind a plain white shower curtain.

Avery winced—welcome to the '60s.

Daisy shrugged. "I know, I know. But considering the house is from the 1920s, I should be thankful it has a bathroom up here at all. It was probably added later."

"Probably. Can you imagine all you kids living here and sharing this one bathroom?"

Daisy laughed. "I never thought about that! Mom and Dad built the other house when I was born, so this one has only ever been a curiosity. Six girls and one bathroom? Poor Hawthorne would have never gotten a shower."

Hawthorne in the shower was something Avery did *not* need to dwell on, and she quickly changed the subject back to the renovations, asking about a giant hole in the ceiling of the bedroom they passed. As Daisy told the ridiculous story of her first meeting with Lance, Avery felt the lightness of true friendship. She never seemed to find that during her final year of high school in Freedom. At college, she had become so caught up with Brandon, friendships hadn't been a priority.

Being back with Daisy and Poppy almost felt like she'd never left. They'd made promises when Avery moved away. But promises to stay in touch at seventeen weren't often kept, even with the help of the internet. Whatever social media site had been the rage when they were young had fallen by the wayside eventually, and virtual friendships were easy to lose sight of. It was refreshing to be back at Bloom's Farm. Even though her age-old crush on Hawthorne would have to remain in the distant past, she wanted to come back. She wouldn't let Hawthorne stop her from rebuilding her ties with the rest of the Bloom family.

5

*A*fter brunch, he escaped as quickly as he could. Nothing was pressing around the farm, but his phone chimed with a text message while he mucked the stall of his horse. Mocha had nuzzled him, excited at the prospect of a ride. Maybe later, but for now Hawthorne put him out in the pasture while he worked.

Brunch this morning had really thrown him for a loop. The last person he'd expected to see walk into his parents' kitchen was the woman from the bar. And to find out that she'd been around from the time he was sixteen until twenty-one was totally mystifying.

Hawthorne had always enjoyed torturing his

sisters and their friends. He'd tried to convince himself it was just a brother's duty, but he had to admit getting the reactions from his sisters' cute friend had been half the fun. Until now, those memories didn't have a name attached to them, but it had always been Avery. He carted the wheelbarrow full of dirty hay to the muck pile and worked to refill Mocha's water and feed while he replayed memories of Avery. Now that they were important, his mind was filling in the details and the hazy scenes had renewed clarity.

One time in particular, when they were fourteen and he was seventeen, he'd just found a snake in the barn and was headed to the creek to let it loose. He spotted Daisy, Andi, Poppy, and Avery laying on towels on their makeshift beach by the creek. With a glint of mischief in his eye, he evaluated his options. Hawthorne tiptoed behind them and dumped the snake between Poppy and Avery with a laugh. Poppy let out an ear-splitting shriek, causing the other girls to jump and start screaming as well. Hawthorne stood back watching, roaring with laughter as the snake traversed the beach towels trying to find an escape.

With a huff, Avery glared at him and marched

over to the snake. "It's just a garter snake, guys," she said while gently straightening the towels under the panicked snake and tipping it toward the long grass at the bank of the creek. Daisy and Poppy were still yelling at him, and Andi came at him, fists flying. But Avery? As he caught a weak blow from Andi, he saw Avery covering a smile behind her fingers. When the ruckus had settled, the girls marched back up the hill to the UTV they used to run around the farm.

She'd always been fearless. Whether it was snakes on the beach, or snakes in a bar—Avery wasn't easily shaken. Surrounded by women his entire life who tended toward the dramatic, Hawthorne was impressed. Honestly, Avery was impressive all around. Smart, capable, kind. A woman like her wouldn't be interested in him. He was just a handyman.

Which didn't matter because he wasn't inter-ested in a relationship. He'd tried the responsibility thing before and had vowed never to do it again. Nobody—not even the alluring Avery Chase—was going to change his mind.

While he placed a new bed of hay in Mocha's stall, he felt the buzz of a text message. After glancing at his phone, his gaze locked longingly on the saddle he'd pulled of the tack room. His shoulders slumped, he wouldn't be going for that ride after all. Leaving Mocha behind and jumping in the truck, he headed out to the event center.

Twenty minutes later, Hawthorne climbed down from the loft in the renovated barn, carrying the giant wooden sign Lily needed for the wedding reception. Lily assured him she wouldn't need anything else, so he made the short walk from the barn to the old house. He needed a shower, probably a shave too. He rubbed a hand over his thickening scruff. After jogging up the porch steps, he pulled the screen door open. A laugh floated out from the kitchen to his right and he froze in the doorway as the screen door slammed behind him.

Avery was here.

A quick glance into the kitchen confirmed his suspicions. Avery and Daisy were sitting at the small table tucked in the corner of the kitchen, each with a Diet Dr. Pepper in hand. At his sudden interruption, Avery sat up straight and stammered.

"I-I should go."

Daisy began to protest, but Avery was already dumping her soda into the sink and gathering her scarf and coat. The motion was so similar to the night in the bar that Hawthorne couldn't restrain himself. He had no intention of confronting Avery. Of course, that was before he realized she intended to ignore him completely.

The words jumped out, "Sure, just run out again without giving me a chance."

Avery raised an eyebrow and he saw Daisy's wide-eyed look of surprise across the room.

Avery held her scarf in one hand and stopped her flurry of activity. "Do you have something you'd like to say, Hawthorne?" She raised her chin and spoke clearly, almost daring him to continue.

He ran a hand through his dark, wind-blown hair. Did he have something to say? Hawthorne could think of a few things, but none of them seemed right. Finally, he answered, "Can I walk you out?" Maybe the words would come to him.

Avery studied him for a second and then turned back to Daisy for a quick hug. "I'll see you and Poppy later this week, okay?"

"Sounds good." Daisy studied them both with a bemused smile before walking behind Avery. "Be nice," she mouthed to Hawthorne. Great, he would hear about this later from everyone.

He extended an arm toward the entry way. "Shall we?"

Avery walked ahead of him out the front door. She stopped abruptly on the porch and turned back toward him. Unable to stop, Hawthorne nearly knocked her over. With a slight grunt at the impact, he steadied her with a hand on her shoulder and froze as she looked up at him. What was he doing? Questions floated in her silvery-gray eyes, but no hint of embarrassment or insecurity.

Admiration filled him. Despite her initial reaction being to flee when he walked in, Avery seemed more than willing to face the remnants of their interaction at the bar. It would be far easier to ignore it forever, and he nearly wished he could.

Hawthorne took a step back to put some desperately needed space between them. "Look, about the bar-" he started.

Avery raised an eyebrow, waiting for him to continue.

"What I mean to say is... I was wrong." Surprise registered on Avery's face and he continued. "I was being a jerk with that story. And you are right — those guys are immature and the way they treated Wendy? Well, I wouldn't want anyone to treat my sisters that way. So, I guess I wanted to say thank you."

Avery paused and bit her lip, causing his eyes to drop at the movement. "You're welcome."

He looked up sharply. Heat climbed up his neck and he cleared his throat. "Yes, well. It's good to see you again, Avery. I know Daisy is glad to have you back in town."

Avery nodded. "And what about you?"

"What?" His brain was having a hard time functioning with her so close. A few short inches and he could finger the blonde hair trailing over the edges of her lightweight scarf.

"Are you glad to have me back?" Her lips formed a sarcastic smirk and he was overwhelmed by the urge to see if his kiss would be capable of ruffling her feathers. As far as he could tell, nothing seemed to get to her. Could he rattle her at all?

Instead, Hawthorne gave a flirty grin, "Well, I guess that depends on what happens next." Almost instinctively, he followed up the suggestive comment with a wink, then mentally winced at his antics. Something about Avery made him want to push her buttons. Even as he said the words, he knew he was fishing on thin ice.

A slight flush filled Avery's cheeks and she fought back a smile while watching his eyes.

Hawthorne smirked. *Rattle rattle.* Then, with a curt nod, she turned and walked down the stairs. As she reached her car, she looked back up at his position on the porch and called out, "Hawthorne?"

"Yeah?"

"Nothing will happen next."

He lifted a hand, then whispered to himself, "We'll see about that, Avery Chase."

His desire to prove her wrong was dangerous. No matter how much he wanted to make her smile, or how desperately he wanted to kiss the sarcastic smirk off her face, he couldn't risk a relationship. Getting under her skin was enjoyable, that was all. He definitely wasn't looking for anything that lasted more than a few weeks. A relationship like that might end in commitment.

He winced at the thought. It wasn't the commitment to a single person that scared him; he would love to have one person to spend his life with. Hawthorne had grown up watching his parents love each other deeply and serve each other without reservation, but to be a husband meant being responsible for a family and taking care of someone else. Once upon a time, he'd been trusted by a whole team of people, and he let every single one of them down.

The thought of Avery looking at him with trust and expectation was alluring but knowing later it would only change to a look of embarrassment and disappointment made him grit his teeth. No, he was better off on his own, puttering around the farm with no real stake in anything.

Hawthorne called Josh later that day to give him an update. "Do you remember Avery Chase?"

Josh thought about it for a moment. "Blonde hair, glasses, kind of awkward? Around my sister's age?"

"That's the one. No glasses anymore. And definitely not awkward." Somewhere in the last thirteen years, Avery had uncovered a whole lot of composure — enough to confront a group of strangers in a bar and stand toe-to-toe with him on the front porch without withering under the scrutiny.

"Okay... Now that we've established the identity of Avery Chase, are you going to tell me why it matters?"

"She's the girl from the bar," Hawthorne explained.

Josh boomed a laugh through the phone, "Oh man, seriously? That's hilarious."

Hawthorne sighed, "No, it's not. She was at family brunch this morning."

"Whoa, seriously? I've never even been invited

to family brunch. And I used to basically live at your house." Josh gave an exaggerated scoff, "Tell your mom I'm offended."

"Yeah, right. I'll be sure to tell her," he said with sarcasm. "Apparently Mom has decided Avery is part of the family since hers is so far away. And she's back to being all buddy-buddy with Daisy and Poppy." He shifted gears. "She was in my house, dude."

Josh laughed. "Oh man. You totally like her."

Crap, Josh was right. Hawthorne rubbed a hand over his now clean-shaved face. "Yeah, I think I do." Oh, he was in big trouble. "But it doesn't matter, because I'm not going to pursue anything. Plus, she thinks I'm a giant tool."

"Or maybe she thinks you are charming and handsome and smart."

"You think so?" Hawthorne asked hopefully.

"No, I don't," Josh quipped, "but she might."

They wrapped up the conversation and Hawthorne thought about Josh's advice. Was what happened in the bar really insurmountable? Oh, it had definitely been bad, but it was mostly his friends, with Hawthorne as an innocent bystander. He grimaced at the memory and revised his train of thought. Okay, maybe not so innocent. It didn't help that he hadn't recognized her, which was not a great first impression. Is it still a first impression if you technically knew the person thirteen years ago?

And the ultimate question—why did he care what Avery thought of him if nothing could happen?

6

*O*n Thursday night, Avery headed back out to the farm. Poppy and Daisy had roped her into a girls' night complete with romantic comedies, junk food, and nail polish. Avery ran her thumb over the tips of her fingers, testing the length of her non-existent fingernails. Nail-biting was a nasty habit, but at least it meant she never had to worry about filing them.

Since the old house was mostly chaos, the girls met at the main house. The walk-out basement had functioned as the central hangout space when they were teenagers—perfect for movies, game nights or birthday parties. As soon as she opened the door, Daisy handed Avery the hot pink and teal caboodle tote covered with stickers and hearts drawn in nail polish. With a quick wave to Laura and Keith sitting in front of the fire, each with their own book, the girls went downstairs with arms full of chips, cookies, and a bottle of Poppy's homemade wine.

Mandy Elliot was downstairs with Poppy and rolled her eyes at Daisy's throwback accessory case. "Honestly, Daisy. Aren't we too old for a caboodle?"

"Speak for yourself. Plus, I saw some for sale the other day at Walmart, believe it or not. The nineties are back, baby!" Daisy replied. Avery smiled at the exchange and went over to give Mandy a hug. Avery worked for Mandy's dad, but hadn't seen her childhood friend since moving back.

Poppy flipped through movies and they chose one. Embracing the nineties theme, they chose a romantic comedy and settled in.

Avery could tell Daisy was just biding her time to ask about the exchange with Hawthorne. After a few too many side glances directed her way, Avery turned to her friend, "Do you have a question?"

Daisy's eyes grew wide, fake innocence painting her face. "Who, me?"

With a roll of her eyes, Avery responded. "Yes, you. You are practically vibrating over there."

Daisy dropped the act and quickly pressed pause on the movie. Poppy looked up with surprise. "Hey!"

"I'll turn it back on in a second. There are more pressing matters. Like exactly what Avery and Hawthorne needed to discuss *privately* after brunch on Saturday."

"Ooooh, I want to know, too," Mandy chimed in.

Avery held up a hand. "Okay, okay. It wasn't like that," she said, referring to Daisy's suggestive tone. "It was no big deal."

"Come on. We all know you had a huge crush on him back in the day."

Avery's mouth dropped open. "You knew?"

Poppy interjected this time. "Of course we knew! Half of our friends had a crush on Hawthorne."

"It's true. I totally did," Mandy admitted. "And if any of you tell Garrett that, I'll vehemently deny it. I bet I can get Lily to back me up." Avery caught the smile Mandy gave to her engagement ring.

"And at brunch? You guys didn't say one word to each other."

Poppy nodded. "I don't even think you looked at each other."

Avery shook her head. "It's no big deal. We ran into each other the other night in Terre Haute."

"Uh-oh." Daisy's tone was serious.

"Uh-oh?" Poppy asked.

Daisy sighed. "Hawthorne lives with me, Poppy. I have a pretty good idea what he's up to. Let's just say he doesn't always make it home until morning, and his clothes smell like smoke and beer a little too often." Daisy turned back to Avery, "What happened when you saw him?"

Avery shrugged. "I didn't actually know it was him at first. There were these guys hitting on the waitress and being all skeevy. I called them out on it and then Hawthorne turned around." Avery closed her eyes. "I may have scolded him a bit. Or a lot, actually," she admitted.

Daisy's laugh rang out merrily and she clapped her hands. "That's amazing. I wish I could have seen the look on his face."

Avery groaned. "That's the worst part. He didn't even recognize me." She covered her face with her hands.

"Seriously?" Mandy asked.

"What a dope," Poppy added.

Avery straightened and looked at her friends. "Anyway, I scolded him and called him by name. And then I walked out."

"Boom, mic drop!" Daisy held out a hand and mimed dropping a handheld microphone.

"It wasn't that great. It was kind of humiliating."

Poppy encouraged her, "Yeah, for him! Come on, you did the right thing, Ave."

Daisy nodded. "For sure." Then, with a tilt of her head, she added, "When did you say this happened?"

"Friday before last." It had been almost two weeks, but Avery would never forget how it had shaken her when Hawthorne turned around and laid his brown eyes on her.

"For what it's worth, I don't think he's gone out with those friends again since that night."

Avery frowned. It didn't mean anything, maybe he was just busy. Daisy said herself this hadn't been an unusual occurrence. Hawthorne made a habit of frequenting bars with the goons she'd seen him with. Staying out all night? Who was he staying with? She cringed and pushed the thought away.

"Whatever. Doesn't matter. Can we just watch the movie? And pass me the cookies, would you?"

Daisy pushed play and Mandy tossed the Oreos to Avery.

A second later, Daisy leaned over and whispered, "He's a good man, Avery."

Instead of responding, Avery grabbed an Oreo and slowly separated the halves, staring at the chocolate and cream in her hand. The movie chattered away in the background, but Avery couldn't bring herself to pay attention. She was too busy thinking about Hawthorne.

He got her so flustered and she didn't like it. On the porch, when he'd turned on the charm? She'd had a hard time walking back to her car. But she couldn't be with Hawthorne. No matter what Daisy said.

HAWTHORNE PARKED the four-wheeler in front of the main house. His truck was still down at the barn, but after helping Rose load up a hog who'd wandered out to the apple orchard, he wanted nothing more than a long, hot shower. Something the dingy blue bathroom in the old house still couldn't provide with its tiny hot water tank. He'd have to remind Daisy about the tankless water heater they'd talked about.

Instead, he trudged up the front step and into his parent's house where he'd lived after the bankruptcy until he moved in with Daisy. Most days, the extra freedom was worth roughing it a little. At least Daisy never gave him a hard time when he pulled up in his truck at 6:00 AM.

His parents were sitting in the living room in front of the fire. Hawthorne should have eaten dinner hours ago, but while his stomach was protesting loudly, his to-do list hadn't gotten the memo. Especially after Rose's call. She was adamant about not calling their Dad. As the youngest, Rose was constantly trying to prove she was ready to take over the animals. Hawthorne wasn't sure she was ready, but more power to her, because he definitely didn't want that job. No matter how badly his dad wanted to give it to him.

"Hey sweetie. How was your day?" His mom's soothing voice greeted him.

"It was fine. Just a little sore and hoping I can take advantage of your hot water supply."

His mom chuckled. "Sure, honey. You can use Poppy and Rose's bathroom up here. Or Lily and Lavender's downstairs." He started to head downstairs as his mom continued, "Daisy and Poppy are downstairs with Avery and Mandy, though!"

Hawthorne stopped short and retraced the two steps he had taken. Upstairs bathroom it was. No need to tempt fate and run into Avery. In fact, he found it hard to concentrate even knowing she was downstairs. Nudging the temperature on the dial hotter, he let steam billow through the small bathroom. He resigned himself to using Poppy's organic body wash, which left him smelling like flowers and lemon. What exactly was organic body wash and why was it necessary? Sometimes his sisters made no sense to him—most of the time, if he was being honest.

Since he didn't have clean clothes, he slipped on his wrinkled jeans and his undershirt. Not ideal, but the alternative was Rose's pink terrycloth bathrobe, and he was pretty sure it wouldn't cover much. Rubbing the towel over his hair, he tossed it in the hamper before flipping on the bathroom fan and opening the door. As it opened, he registered Avery's surprised face in front of him.

"Oh!" She flushed, "I'm sorry, I didn't know you were in here."

Hawthorne stared at her and was struck by how beautiful Avery was. Unlike the guarded, irritated look he had received from her, Avery's face was relaxed and joyful. Then she grinned, and he caught the slight purple stains on her teeth from the wine they must be drinking downstairs.

The silence stretched on and words escaped him. Finally, he swallowed and greeted her, "Hey."

She giggled and he couldn't fight the smile.

Avery was edging toward tipsy and it was adorable. "Hey, yourself."

He shifted to one side, "Did you need in?"

"What? Oh, yeah. Daisy was using the one downstairs, so Poppy said I could..." Avery looked up at him and her words trailed off. Then, without warning, Avery leaned in close—her nose at chest level and brushing against his white T-shirt. Then, in a move that was as shocking as it was stirring, she inhaled deeply and made a soft, contented noise Hawthorne would trade his truck to hear her make again.

Hawthorne's mind went completely blank. Thankfully, some self-preservation instinct must have kicked in, because he found himself moving away unconsciously.

Avery must have realized what she'd done because her eyes grew wide and she started to stammer. Her cheeks flushed scarlet and she looked down at the floor. "I-I'm so... It was the lemon," she explained.

So, this was a flustered Avery. This woman was likely to bring him to his knees, if this short interaction was any sign. With a gentle finger, he lifted her chin to meet his gaze. "No problem at all, Avery." Then, he stepped in close again and increased the angle of her chin. He lowered his head, and her eyes fell closed. Just a few seconds more and—

"Oh, Avery. I forgot Hawthorne was using—" his mom's voice came around the corner and stopped abruptly. Avery jumped away from him and he hung his head, cheeks burning in shame and disappointment. Irritation flashed at the interruption before being replaced with guilt at his behavior.

"Yep, he just finished up." Avery's tone was forcefully bright and she ducked into the bathroom and closed the door, leaving him in the hallway to face his mother.

7

*A*very sat on the edge of the bathtub and buried her face in her hands. What had she been thinking? She'd only had half a glass of wine, but clearly Poppy's homemade vintage packed a punch. Or else, there was another something that had her all muddled.

Or another someone.

Hawthorne had her all tied up in knots. The heat climbed up her neck again at the memory of her actions in the hallway. She'd behaved like a cat who wanted to curl up on his lap. Another groan escaped as she rubbed her eyes, then she took a deep breath. It had been close, but nothing had happened. Thank God Mrs. Bloom had come around the corner; the absolute last thing she needed was to kiss Hawthorne Bloom.

After Avery was done and had wallowed in her embarrassment long enough, she opened the door and peeked out, half expecting Hawthorne to ambush her. Or worse—his mother. The coast was clear. She walked as quietly as she could across the living room, past Mr. Bloom dozing in the recliner with an open book laid across his chest. A light snore escaped and she smiled. Miss Laura was notably absent, as was Hawthorne.

Avery sighed with relief at the bottom of the stairs. Her friends were sitting on the floor now, pulling out nail polish from the make-up case, none the wiser about what had nearly transpired between her and their brother just moments before.

She let Mandy paint her nubby fingernails and tried her best not to reveal how jittery she was. Avery felt her phone vibrate in the pocket of her jeans, but her wet fingernails meant waiting to look at it.

It buzzed again two minutes later, and Daisy lifted her head. "Want me to grab that for you?"

Avery tried to play it cool. "Nah, I'm sure it's just my sister or something." *Liar,* her conscience chimed.

"Oh, how is Brie these days?"

"She's good. Still living in Colorado. She works at the mountain resort outside of town." Avery shrugged. "She seems to like it."

Finally- an excruciatingly long five minutes later- Avery pulled the phone out of her pocket. A text from an unfamiliar number showed on the screen.

We need to talk.

Avery, please don't ignore me.

Her heart accelerated as Avery realized Hawthorne had texted her and tapped out a reply. How had he gotten her number? Miss Laura had it, but surely, he hadn't asked his mother!

Nothing to talk about.

Maybe he would give up. Wasn't that what she wanted? Unable to resist, she kept glancing at her phone every few minutes for the next half hour. Avery tried to convince herself it was good that he hadn't replied, because they had no business texting or talking. Or kissing in the hallway.

Still, she glanced at her phone again.

It vibrated and she grabbed it from between her legs with superhuman speed.

Tomorrow night? Shooters at 7?

Quickly, she tapped a reply saying she had a

date. Who was he to assume she was free on a Friday night? But her conscience twinged at the lie and she deleted it.

Fine. But you are buying me mozzarella sticks.

His response was immediate this time.

Deal.

Drive safely tonight.

Her heart warmed at his thoughtfulness, and she realized she was in big trouble. With a surreptitious glance at Daisy and Poppy, she tucked her phone away again. Avery wasn't ready to talk about it with them; after all, tomorrow night could end any number of ways. Mostly, she was afraid it would end with her kicking Hawthorne in the shin for flirting with the waitress. She'd been there, done that with her boyfriend from college. Much younger and less confident, Avery had let it slide and it had turned into a pattern of cheating and disrespect she never wanted to repeat. She wasn't a pushover. She deserved someone committed and serious.

Could Hawthorne be that person? Avery was starting to think maybe he could. But she was reserving the right to change her mind.

~

HAWTHORNE TAPPED the table with the edge of the cardboard coaster. Waiting on a woman wasn't something he was very familiar with, unless you counted his sisters. Daisy especially was almost always running late. Then, Avery opened the door and unwound the scarf from around her neck. He held up an arm to get her attention and when she spotted him and a smile filled her face, he felt his own smile broaden.

Avery slid into the chair across from him. "Hey, sorry I'm late. I got caught by an undergrad who wanted to review every single topic from my lecture before the test next week."

Hawthorne wasn't sure the student's motivation was so innocent. If Avery's students were anything like Hawthorne in college, they had way more than chemistry on the brain. "No problem, I'm just glad you made it. Can I buy you a drink?"

"I'll stick with iced tea."

Hawthorne nodded and ordered two iced teas. With a wink at Avery, he added an order of mozzarella sticks. Before Wendy left, he added "Oh, and Wendy?"

Their waitress looked at him with a raised eyebrow.

"I'm sorry about the way my friends—and I—treated you. You deserve better."

Wendy relaxed and gave a small smile. "Thanks."

"Have they been back without me? I can talk to them if you need me to."

She shook her head. "No, I think your friend here pretty much scared them away." Wendy gestured to Avery with her pen and added, "Thanks for that, by the way."

"Anytime," Avery replied.

Wendy looked at each of them curiously and said, "I'll put your appetizer in and be right back with your drinks."

As Wendy turned away, Avery studied him. "So?"

"So," he replied.

"What are we doing here?" Avery didn't sound unkind, more curious than anything.

"Well," he began, "I thought we should talk."

"I got that much." Avery's sarcasm made him smile.

"Yeah, okay. Here's the thing: my mom about tanned my hide last night after she saw us in the hallway." The truth was his mom had all but grabbed him by the ear and pulled him onto the back deck, where he proceeded to freeze his toes off while she lectured him about respect and boundaries.

Avery flushed and closed her eyes. "I'm so embarrassed. I never should have—"

"You didn't do anything, Avery," he interrupted. "The truth is," he paused and gathered the courage to say what he'd been practicing mentally all day, "I don't really date much, but I like you. A lot."

Avery's eyes grew wide and she let out a breath. "Wow. That's not exactly what I was expecting."

Seriously? Had she not been in the same hallway he had last night? "Really? What did you expect?"

"I'm not sure. But it wasn't that." Avery waved her hands, gesturing to the busy bar. "I sort of figured you were bringing me here to let me down gently or ask me to stay away from the farm."

Hawthorne furrowed his brow. "What? Why would you need to stay away from the farm? You're always welcome there."

"Okay..." After a long hesitation, she continued, "Hawthorne, this isn't a good idea."

He felt his brow furrow and replied, "What do you mean?"

"You and me. We're not a good idea." With her clarification, Hawthorne felt his stomach lurch.

He leaned toward her across the small table,

"Why not? I like you, and I think you like me too. Unless my signals are all mixed up, I'm pretty sure you *wanted* me to kiss you last night."

Avery flushed, "That's not the point. The point is that I'm not looking for something casual."

Hawthorne interjected with a shake of his head, "Neither am I."

Avery looked at him with a raised eyebrow. "You're not? You're looking for marriage and kids and the whole shebang? Because that's what I'm waiting for." She watched his face and must have seen the panic he was desperately trying to stuff back down. "That's what I thought." Avery stepped off her bar stool and Hawthorne laid a hand on her arm.

"Just wait, Avery. Give me a chance." It felt an awful lot like begging, which made him feel pathetic and he pulled his arm back.

A long moment later, where Hawthorne felt like the fate of the world rested on the outcome, Avery softened and sat back down. "I'll stay until the mozzarella sticks are gone." At the victory on his face, she added, "But only because I haven't eaten anything since breakfast."

Hawthorne sighed with relief. Why did the thought of her walking away scare him so much? Her concerns were valid, he'd give her that. But he had about seven minutes until the appetizer. Could he convince her to give him a second chance at a first impression? "Can I tell you a story while we wait?"

Wendy dropped off their drinks, and after Avery agreed, Hawthorne started from the beginning.

"During college, I started a company. It took off and by six months after graduation, I had fourteen full-time employees and a handful of six-figure investors." At her surprised look, Hawthorne felt the traitorous swell of pride. Wouldn't it be nice if that was where the story ended?

"We were doing great, but got overextended." Hawthorne rubbed a hand over his face, and admitted the worst part, "The company went bankrupt and people lost their jobs. I couldn't even pay everyone their last paychecks." His voice broke and he swallowed painfully. "I let them all down."

He looked up, trying to read Avery's face and seeing only compassion. "I had no idea, Hawthorne."

It wasn't exactly something he advertised, but he bit back the sarcastic comment. In many ways, that chapter of his life had been an Indiana tornado, tearing through quickly and leaving a trail of destruction in its wake. Hawthorne shrugged, "I really don't talk about it much. It's been ten years, which seems like a long time when I say it out loud. But the idea of having people rely on me again... Even thinking about it makes me want to hide in the hayloft."

With a small smile, Avery laid her hand across the table over his. "That must have been hard to go through."

That was putting it lightly. At the time, he felt like the biggest failure. He still did, most of the time. Hawthorne ducked his head, embarrassed at the admission. Avery was quiet for a moment and he studied her delicate hand resting on his, dirt and grease still staining the edges of his fingernails. He flipped his hand so it rested palm-to-palm with hers.

Quietly, Avery broke the comfortable silence, her fingers twisting with his, "So what now?"

Hawthorne looked up from their interlocked fingers. "What do you mean?"

"If you are scared to let someone count on you again, what do you see happening here?" Avery's eyes were kind but imploring. "I've been with someone I couldn't rely on, and I'm not making that mistake again."

Dozens of questions sprang to mind, his desire to know more about her story overwhelming him. Who hurt her? The image of Avery hurt and broken, the exact opposite of the strong woman he'd seen since she came home, flashed before him. Is that what he would do to her?

He had to believe he wouldn't. Otherwise, Hawthorne was destined to watch her find happiness with someone else.

"Avery, I'm terrified of letting someone down again." Especially her, if his racing pulse and rolling stomach were any indication. "It was the worst thing I've ever experienced. But at the same time, I don't want to let you go."

Avery shook her head in response, "I can't be your experiment." She pulled her hand away, and the loss of contact cooled his hand and his confidence. He stared at his now empty palm and felt the absence of her hand as though his own had been cut off.

Swallowing nervously, he spoke the only words that came to mind. "I'm not going anywhere," he told her.

Avery smiled, "Neither am I."

A glimmer of hope flashed. If he wanted Avery, it would mean stepping up. Not only for her, but for his family and the farm. Was he ready to do that?

He watched Avery pull a string of melted mozzarella away from her lips, a smile tugging at his own. If there had ever been a woman worth working for, it was her.

8

*P*oppy came to him a few days later, nervously twisting her rings around her fingers.

Glancing up from the tractor tire he was inspecting, he raised an eyebrow. "Spill it, Poppy."

"I need to get away for a day or two."

He straightened in surprise and grabbed a rag to wipe his hands. "For what?"

Poppy looked down, "I can't say. But I need someone to keep an eye on things for me." She looked up at him, almost a full head taller. "Lewis and Clint know everything that needs done, but if anything happens... Could you just run things around here for a few days?"

Hawthorne frowned. This was an unusual

request, far outside his normal responsibilities. "What about Dad?" he asked.

Poppy's shoulders sagged. "I was hoping not to bring Mom and Dad into this." Then, his sister turned away, her cotton skirt twirling around her boots. "It's fine. Forget I asked."

The conversation with Avery echoed in his mind. Maybe it was time for him to face his fear. "Wait, wait. I'll do it." Maybe this was an answer to prayer. He'd been diving into his Bible in the evenings since he stopped heading to town every night. He had no idea how to make it happen, but he'd been praying for God to help him see how he could move beyond the hang-ups from his past.

Poppy sighed with relief as he continued, "But you owe me. And I expect to hear what this is all about sooner rather than later," he gave her a pointed look. She grinned and a scary thought hit him, "You're not eloping with some guy, right?"

Poppy scoffed at him, "Who would I run away with? You know I haven't been seeing anyone." Then, she stepped in close and wrapped her arms around him. He held the dirty rag away from her and patted her shoulder. "Thanks, Hawthorne."

"Yeah, yeah. Just be careful with whatever you're doing." The protective big-brother instinct never really went away—even when his sisters were nearly thirty themselves. At least Poppy was pretty level-headed. If it had been Lavender or Daisy coming to him with some suspicious story about leaving home for a few days, he would have gone into interrogation mode.

He already knew Clint and Lewis, Poppy's farmhands, but he and Poppy tracked them down in the field harvesting the last of the pumpkins and winter squash. After letting them know Hawthorne would be their main contact for the next few days, Poppy went back to the main house to pack a bag.

Even though he hadn't expected it to be difficult, Hawthorne was still surprised how easy it was to be the boss over the next few days. There was a surge of energy that came with being the decision-maker. Clint came to him with questions about the apple orchard, since the season was almost over, and the pick-your-own apple events had ended. It was an easy call to make for Hawthorne, and he told Clint to pick the rest of the apples that were good. If he knew his sister at all, Poppy would want to make apple butter to sell next year.

Then, he had them take any half-rotten apples over to the animal barn, since he knew Rose always needed more food for the pigs. Those darn animals would eat literally anything you gave them. At Rose's surprised reaction, he gathered that wasn't something they'd ever done before. The simple exchange got him thinking about other ways different portions of the farm could support each other.

Before he made it too far down that line of thought though, Poppy returned and took back her office, dodging his questions about her impromptu disappearance. He'd helped a few others while she was gone—a minor computer issue for Lavender and a leaky faucet at the event barn.

When he stopped by the bed and breakfast and heard Daisy arguing with Lance, her new contractor, he couldn't help but step in to mediate.

Lance spoke first, gesturing wildly with a tape measure in hand. "Tell your sister that it is crazy to have a commercial size refrigerator and stove for a bed and breakfast that will serve eight people one meal a day!"

Daisy stomped her foot, her nose sprinkled with drywall dust. "Tell Lance that I'm not paying him to criticize my plans."

Lance sputtered and Hawthorne held up a hand. "Whoa, whoa, whoa. Take a minute, you two." Then he shook his head. "I don't know what's going on here; I could have sworn you were finally getting along." Hawthorne narrowed his eyes at his sister and Daisy tucked her chin.

He looked at Lance, "Tell me why it's a bad idea." When Daisy tried to jump in, he held up a finger to silence her, "Let the man talk, Daze."

Lance explained the extra cost of electrical work for the larger appliances and the cost of the appliances themselves. With a nod, Hawthorne turned to his sister. "And why do you want the commercial-grade equipment?"

Daisy cast a vision for a commercial kitchen where a chef could prepare and serve a breakfast that garnered rave reviews. She was convinced a high-quality kitchen would help attract a high-quality chef. As she spoke, Hawthorne's own strategic mind took off.

He looked at Lance and waved a thumb toward Daisy. "I'm with her on this one." Daisy jumped up and pointed triumphantly at her contractor before Hawthorne interrupted her celebration, "Not for the reasons you said, sis."

She glared at him, but a hint of curiosity was etched on her face. "Why, then?"

Hawthorne explained, "We've got to think big picture. With the event center and the bed and breakfast, we would have more than enough work to keep a chef busy. And they wouldn't be serving eight people once per day. They could be serving two hundred people three times a week, which means a commercial kitchen would be exactly what they need. Plus," he continued, "Poppy could grow her canning and prepared foods business if she had a kitchen other than Mom and Dad's."

It seemed so obvious how they could leverage their talent, space, and access to customers and take Bloom's Farm to the next level.

Lance nodded. *"That* makes sense," he conceded. To Daisy, he said, "You win. On a technicality."

"I'll take it," she said before floating up the stairs.

Hawthorne asked Lance about the renovations and teased him about dealing with Daisy.

Lance shook his head, "I don't know how you live with her. She wears me out."

Hawthorne chuckled, "I don't think she puts nearly as much energy into antagonizing me as she does you." His sister was a fireball, for sure. It was no wonder Lance's methodical, controlled nature was clashing with Daisy's ready-shoot-aim approach. If nothing else, the fireworks were fun to watch.

The chemistry he could see erupting between his sister and the unsuspecting contractor had him thinking of Avery. Oh, they had the chemistry side of things covered, but maybe he was finally embracing some of the responsibility he needed to prove himself to Avery. In just a few days, he'd created new opportunities for the farm to work more efficiently. While Poppy was gone, he'd been the person making the decisions—and he didn't hate it. Actually, it was freeing to let out the ideas he'd been burying.

All this time, had he been fooling himself thinking it was better to be the handyman, available from eight to five and only doing what was asked? He'd forgotten how fun it had been at the pinnacle of the company's success to look at the processes and unite the team behind a vision.

It didn't feel like enough, though. Not enough to call Avery and tell her. A few measly ideas and a two-day stint as the fill-in supervisor over the farmhands? That wasn't responsibility, but it was a start. And it felt good.

Hawthorne stopped by the main house a few days later to talk with his dad. He caught him in the kitchen, making coffee. It was something his dad did every morning, even though he didn't drink it himself and only made it to bring a cup to his mom. "What brings you here this early?" his dad asked.

Hawthorne swallowed his nervousness. "Well, I

figured it would be good for us to catch up a bit over breakfast. Maybe see how I can help."

His dad scooped coffee grounds into the filter, "Hawthorne, you do plenty already."

"I know I help out," he shook his head, "but I sometimes feel like the things I'm doing could easily be done by anyone. Shouldn't I be doing more?"

Keith raised an eyebrow in surprise. "Do you want to do more?"

Hawthorne jerked a shoulder, "I don't know. Maybe?"

"I thought after..." his dad waved a hand as he trailed off.

Hawthorne knew what he was referring to and filled in the blanks, "You mean, after I bankrupted my company and put fourteen people out of a job?"

His dad shrugged, "Well, yeah. That."

Hawthorne sighed, "I'm not saying I want that kind of responsibility again, because I don't. But maybe I could do a bit more here."

"Most of what needs done is the general manager stuff. Payroll, taxes, annual planning. Thank God for your mother. I never would have managed all the financial work without her. Now, mostly what I do around here is just make sure we don't shoot ourselves in the foot."

Hawthorne cringed. "Like I did, you mean?"

Realizing his gaff, Keith flinched and turned to his son. "That's not what I was saying—"

Hawthorne felt the fire in his cheeks and his pulse rising in embarrassment. He cut off his father's explanation, not wanting to hear any more. "It's fine, Dad. If you don't want my help, I'll just keep doing my own thing and whatever else my sisters need." The chair he'd been sitting in scraped noisily against the floor as he stood. "I think Lily needs some help tearing down from the banquet the other night." He spoke over his father's objections, ducking out the door just as he heard his father's call.

"Hawthorne, wait!"

9

*A*very thought about declining when Mandy invited Avery to the wedding. Even though she'd been able to catch up with her at the girls' night, it had been years since she'd seen her childhood friend before that.

Still, the invitation clipped to her refrigerator mocked her, the location marked as "Bloom's Farm Storybook Barn". If she went, she might run into Hawthorne. She remembered him and Josh being thick as thieves, but she couldn't figure out if the potential Hawthorne sighting was a mark in the pro or the con column of her decision-making process.

Avery knew Daisy was in the wedding and the others would be there, too. Plus, anything was better than another evening spent at her apartment reading.

She was definitely not going so she could see Hawthorne. Just in case, though, Avery spent a little extra time perfecting her makeup and retrieved the dreaded spandex shapewear from the back of her closet. She wanted to look good in the pictures, that was all. Certainly not trying to impress anyone.

Regardless of her motives, Avery was glad she'd decided to attend. Storybook Barn was something magical when everything came together. Small twinkle lights and white, gauzy fabric made the old-fashioned barn seem elegant and romantic. It was the perfect combination of every trendy wedding blog Avery had run across in the last ten years. She said as much to Lily, who was somehow balancing being a guest and coordinator. There must have been some sort of emergency, because Avery spotted Mandy's brother, Josh, having an animated conversation with Lily before the couple's first dance.

As Mandy and Dr. Pike cut the cake after the dance, Avery ducked outside to avoid the inevitable bouquet toss. The last thing she wanted was to be paraded in front of everyone with every other single woman. Ugh.

Avery stared out over the rolling hills dotted with round hay bales, admiring the view of the farm as muted music played over the muffled voice of the DJ in the barn behind her. The night was chilly, though, and she rubbed her bare arms, wishing she'd thought to grab her shawl from the back of her chair. Silky, warm fabric was laid across her shoulders and she caught the familiar scent of lemon.

"Beautiful wedding, wasn't it?" From behind her right shoulder, Hawthorne's quiet voice flooded her with warmth down to her toes, exposed in black peep-toe heels. Avery pulled his suit jacket tighter and nodded, glancing over her shoulder to drink in a glimpse of him. Somehow, she hadn't seen him all night. Not that she'd been searching the crowd or anything.

Working at the farm in flannel shirts and jeans, Hawthorne was handsome. In a casual, collared shirt at the bar, he was downright distracting. Tonight, in a dress shirt and tie, clean-shaved and perfectly put-together? Hawthorne was positively jaw-dropping, and she felt her heart rate accelerate at the sight of him.

Afraid to be caught staring, Avery turned back to the fields and searched for something to say, anything to fracture the moment. "Quite the view, isn't it?" Seriously? That was the best she could come up with? He lived here, for crying out loud!

She felt him step closer, his breath on her neck. "Yes, you really are quite stunning," he replied.

A shiver crawled up Avery's spine and she resisted the urge to squirm in response to it. She closed her eyes and inhaled the tangy lemon scent of him, momentarily back in the hallway, her inhibitions weakened.

"Avery—" he started and her breath hitched, "It's good to see you." Hawthorne cleared his throat and added, "Dance with me?"

She turned then, needing to see his eyes. Barely six inches stood between them; Avery looked up at him. Her gaze traced his features, falling from his dark eyes, along his jawline and landing on his lips. As she watched they twitched, and she looked back up with a blink. What would he do if she asked him to kiss her?

Hawthorne closed his eyes with a groan, and for a moment, Avery wondered if she'd spoken her last thought out loud. Hawthorne shifted his weight and laid a palm on her cheek. Instinctively, she pressed into the warmth of his skin.

Accepting his earlier invitation, she pulled her hands from the pockets of his suit jacket and placed one on his shoulder and joined the other with his, immediately missing the feel of his skin on her cheek.

They danced slowly to the music playing inside, the sound muffled by the closed barn doors. Unable to resist, she inhaled deeply near his neck.

"What's with the lemon?" she asked, curiously.

He looked down with a blush and her heart melted. "I, um, stole it from Poppy after you..." he cleared his throat again. "In the hallway," he clarified, "you seemed to like it."

Avery hummed noncommittally. Hawthorne was right, but she wasn't going to embarrass herself by admitting how happy it made her that he'd changed his soap to appeal to her. His hand rested gently on her waist, holding her close, burning her skin even through the jacket, dress, and the awful spandex contraption she'd squeezed into.

She looked up at him, his jawline just beyond the reach of her lips. Then, he looked down at her, creating precious few inches between them to meet her eyes. The music faded as her pulse thundered in her ears and their gentle swaying stopped altogether. Her eyes drifted closed and she lifted her face to his, a silent invitation.

The warm whisper of his lips on her cheek brought every ounce of the building anticipation crashing over her. Disappointment flared and she stepped back, needing air. Had she read the signals wrong?

Her eyes met his. The desire she saw there left her stomach fluttering like the tiny bubbles from champagne toast. Definitely reading the right signals.

"Tell me it's different now," she pleaded in a whisper. Being this close to him was muddling her resolve. Avery wanted him to convince her that he was ready, and then she wanted him to kiss her.

He met her gaze with apologetic eyes. "I'm still working on it, Avery." Logically, she knew it had only been a few weeks, and that wasn't enough time. Daisy may insist that something was happening with Hawthorne, but Avery couldn't be sure. But that didn't change the very illogical portion of her brain that was crying out for her to ignore her better judgement.

Looking down, Hawthorne rubbed a hand through his hair, He glanced back up at her, with pleading eyes. "Just don't give up on me yet, okay?"

———

10

*T*hanksgiving was only a few weeks away now and Avery considered flying out to visit her parents in Colorado, but Freedom would be busy with the influx of winter tourists for ski season. Freedom Ridge Resort was a favorite winter destination of people from all over the country, and her parents loved the small, tourist town. Avery, on the other hand, had been more than ready to leave after graduation.

Instead, Avery accepted the invitation to have Thanksgiving at Bloom's Farm. She hadn't heard much from Hawthorne since the wedding. The lack of communication hadn't stopped her from thinking about him, though; almost incessantly. With every text message from Daisy, Avery stopped herself from asking about him. If Hawthorne was ready to commit and still interested in her, surely he would reach out. It had been two months since they met at Shooter's.

Hawthorne said he wasn't going anywhere, but maybe he'd changed his mind. Still, she was determined not to pin her hopes on a leopard changing his spots. When Edward from the chemistry department asked her again to join him for dinner, she agreed.

Which is how she found herself wanting to stab herself in the eye with a salad fork, listening to Edward drone on about the dangers of natural gas drilling.

The server cleared her salad plate, taking the potential rescue weapon with him, and Avery debated the merits of using a butter knife instead. "Can I get you another glass of wine, ma'am?"

Edward responded for her, "That would be grand, thank you." He drew out the words, his pretentious tone making Avery want to roll her eyes.

As the server reached for the empty wineglass, Avery covered the rim with her hand. "No, thank you. I'll just take a glass of water." One glass was more than enough, or she'd be asleep before the main course arrived. She'd agreed to go out with Edward because he was cute, in a bookworm sort of way, and he'd always been personable and kind enough, if a little dry.

Sitting at a quiet table in the fanciest restaurant in Terre Haute though, Avery questioned her own sanity. She excused herself and walked toward the ladies' room, hoping she could kill a few minutes and praying that when she returned the food would be there. It would certainly be the only highlight of the evening.

Avery sighed at herself in the mirror. Dating was the worst. Truth be told, there was nothing wrong with Edward. Perhaps he was a touch boring and a bit too political for her, but he was nice enough. It made telling him she wasn't interested difficult.

She couldn't help but wish Hawthorne was the one sitting across the table from her. Avery knew they'd spend the evening bantering and laughing, probably poking fun at the upscale menu that described simple fries as 'hand-seasoned, fried, julienned potatoes'. If Hawthorne was waiting for her at the table, she would hurry back, instead of using the hand dryer until her hands were fully dry and scrolling through her text messages one last time.

Unable to resist, Avery sent a quick text to

Hawthorne and tucked her phone away. Then, she went back to her date. Maybe when the date was over and she'd let Edward down easy, she'd have a message in her inbox from the man who'd been on her mind the whole night.

HAWTHORNE SMILED as he read Avery's message under the table. His pulse kicked up a notch with the knowledge that he would see her in a few weeks. He only wished he'd thought of extending the invitation for Thanksgiving himself. His mother had apparently seen to it for him though.

He glanced up to see his mom watching him with smile. "Everything okay, sweetie?"

Hawthorne cleared his throat and nodded, jumping back to the conversation at hand. "Like I said, I've been thinking a lot about my role here at the farm."

Keith nodded, "You know we appreciate everything you do."

"I know, Dad. But I really think I'm ready to do more." His mom beamed and he smiled in return. "I'll never be able to thank you enough for your support after the bankruptcy. Honestly, I didn't think it would be as hard as it was to see what I'd built be torn apart limb from limb."

Watching his company be dismantled to pay off debts had been excruciating. But it wasn't nearly as hard as the meeting he'd held with his loyal employees, letting them know the doors were closing and they should look for a new job.

Hawthorne continued, "I've realized that my strengths at the company were the big picture and the processes. The interaction of all the moving pieces. And," he looked at his dad, "I think I can bring some of that here." He went on to explain his vision for Daisy's kitchen and catering for the event center. And how the produce Poppy grew could support not only the menu for those, but provide scraps for the animals as well.

"I think we are missing chances for Bloom's Farm to work together, instead of as isolated business units. And I'd like to head up the effort to improve," he finished. He was taking on a project, which a start to his whole new take on responsibility. No one would lose their job if he failed, but it was something he could put his name on and claim as his own. He hadn't done that in a long time.

Keith reached an arm over and dropped a heavy

hand on Hawthorne's shoulder. "Well, now, that sounds like a perfect job for you." Then, his deep voice thick with emotion, "I'm proud of you, Hawthorne."

Hawthorne warmed at the praise. "Thanks, Dad. I'm excited to see what we can do."

Then, his mom chimed in, "I'm excited to see what you can do, sweetie." Quietly, she added, "You've been hiding here for too long."

Hawthorne nodded. He had been hiding—from responsibility. As the floating handyman, success was measured on a small scale. Did he find the missing sheep? Did he fix the fence or change the tire? A project like this meant success in bigger terms: would he make the farm more efficient? Would he grow business by creating new opportunities? Or would he waste his time and spend money they shouldn't?

With his company, his vision had been bigger than his cash flow. The last thing he wanted was to let that happen again. Ideas were one thing—signing checks and hiring staff was another. He didn't know if he was there yet.

Another text message chimed in his pocket. Avery. Even more than he'd wanted to share his new ideas with his parents and get them on board with his new role, he wanted to tell Avery. He'd call her after dinner and, if nothing else, he would get to see her soon for Thanksgiving. That thought had him smiling through the rest of dinner.

Avery successfully navigated the 'no second date' conversation at the tail end of dinner, convinced Edward to let her pay for her own meal, and made it back to the fuzzy, fleece pajamas that waited for her at home. She sighed deep into the corner of the couch and flipped on the TV as her phone lit up on the coffee table with a buzz.

Hawthorne.

She'd checked her phone in the car immediately after her date ended, stifling disappointment when her only new message was from Brielle. Eagerly, she reached for the phone and felt her cheeks burn with a grin at Hawthorne's name displayed on the notification bubble.

Before she could over-analyze her own actions, she hit the call button, instead of responding to his question.

His throaty chuckle hummed in her ear after the connection clicked. "I guess that's a yes."

She blushed and tucked her legs under a blanket. "I'm awake," she confirmed.

They hadn't talked on the phone before and she swore she could feel the deep vibration of his voice all the way to her toes when he responded, "I'm glad."

Hawthorne asked how her week had been, and Avery couldn't help but tease him a bit. She chose her words carefully, "It was good. Students are practically buzzing with the upcoming break, but I had a date tonight to look forward to." There, that was accurate. She really had been looking forward to the date—until it started.

Avery heard him cough and smiled to herself. "Oh, I didn't realize you were seeing someone." The unasked question was evident in his voice.

She debated how long to let him wonder but couldn't bring herself to be dishonest. "It was a first date, and it turned out to be a major bust."

Hawthorne didn't sound too disappointed as he expressed his sympathy. Or was she just imagining it because she wanted him to be a little jealous?

"We haven't talked much lately; how have you been?" Avery asked.

Hawthorne grew more animated as he talked about the project he would be leading at Bloom's

Farm. This was the kind of passion had been absent from him before. The excitement in his voice as he spoke about the ideas he'd already implemented was contagious, and she found herself asking questions and encouraging him.

Why was this so different than listening to Edward drone on about natural gas drilling? Hawthorne stopped and apologized for dominating the conversation, and she realized the difference.

This was Hawthorne.

She'd gladly listen to him talk about anything he was passionate about. Avery only wished the conversation was happening in person so she could see the fire in his eyes. It was an added bonus that this seemed to be a major step forward for Hawthorne, something intentional, proving he was more than a cavalier cad working for a paycheck until the next night at the bar.

"That's really amazing, Hawthorne. I'm proud of you," she said with a smile.

"You know what? I'm proud of me too. But enough about me—tell me why you chose chemical engineering."

Avery laughed, "Really? That's the burning question you have for me?"

"What?" Hawthorne replied with mock woundedness. "I want to know everything, Avery. You just seemed to disappear after I went to college." She blushed, the low timbre of his voice making her want to melt into the couch cushions.

"Oh yeah, right. It's not like you remember me from back then."

"Sure, I do," he insisted. "You were always hanging around the twins and Poppy."

That much was true, she thought. Daisy and Dandelion were her best friends, and Poppy was only a year younger. The four of them, along with Mandy Elliot, had always been together. "Okay, if you remember me so well, tell me something."

Her smug smile grew with the silence as she waited. Then, her mouth fell open as he spoke, "I remember eavesdropping on a game of Truth or Dare you were playing in the barn."

Avery laughed. "You did not!"

A low chuckle filtered through the phone. "Oh yes, we did. Josh and I were in the loft when the five of you came in. It was," he paused, "enlightening."

She covered her face, thinking of the potentially embarrassing actions the fourteen-year-old version of herself had committed.

He continued, "And in case you need more

proof, I'll just say that your willingness to capture and kiss a toad was inspiring."

Her face burned. "I can't believe you saw that," she laughed. "Though, he certainly wasn't the last toad I kissed," she said, thinking of the boyfriends she'd had in high school and college.

"Well, I remember being impressed. The other girls shrieked and squealed like it was the end of the world."

"Andi never squealed a day in her life," Avery corrected.

Hawthorne conceded. "That's probably true. But the others did. Most of them chose truth every time, but not you."

"Good thing I didn't," Avery mused.

"Oh?" Hawthorne's curiosity was evident in his voice.

Whoops, she didn't mean to go there. But she answered him anyway. "I stopped choosing truth because your sisters always asked who I had a crush on and teased me when I wouldn't answer."

Then, he asked the question she both hoped he wouldn't and prayed he would, "Why wouldn't you answer the question?"

"Because the answer was always you." She

closed her eyes and held her breath, waiting for his response.

Hawthorne cleared his throat, "And what about now?"

Avery exhaled with relief and a loud laugh escaped. She grinned at the ceiling and answered, "I'll let you know."

11

When Poppy invited her to join her at the Minden Fall Festival, Avery hadn't considered what they would be doing. The Bloom's Farm "Pumpkin Patch" was set up in the park, with a hundred pumpkins of various sizes spread out in piles and on straw bales for children to pick. Avery also hadn't expected Hawthorne to be there helping. She wouldn't complain about watching him haul the heavy pumpkins from the truck while she and Poppy arranged them.

"How about we trade jobs?" Hawthorne stretched after setting a particularly large pumpkin next to a small bale of straw. "I'll add the cutesy flowers and ribbon and you ladies can carry the goods."

Poppy raised an eyebrow at her brother. "I believe this was our deal. I recall someone losing a little bet about catching chickens. Winner got out of carting pumpkins," she explained to Avery, who covered her mouth to hide a giggle.

Hawthorne grinned, "Well, Avery should have to help. I didn't see her catch any chickens."

Avery's mouth fell open with a laugh, "I wasn't even there!" She looked to Poppy for help, but she just looked on with a smile. So much for looking out for a friend. "Seriously? You are going to invite me and then force me into manual labor?"

Poppy shrugged. "He's right. You didn't catch any chickens."

Avery looked back at Hawthorne, saw his devious smile and couldn't help but give in. Working alongside him didn't sound so bad. Then he sealed the deal with his next statement. "I'll buy you a caramel apple afterward."

"Make it a funnel cake and you've got a deal." He smiled his agreement and they spent the next twenty minutes carrying the pumpkins from the trailer to their little patch of grass.

Determined not to let her heavy breathing give away how out of shape she was, she asked Hawthorne questions to keep him talking. He chatted about his projects at the farm, gave her updates on Daisy's renovation and flirted mercilessly. All the heavy lifting had them both working up a sweat and Hawthorne slipped out of his coat, revealing a soft, flannel shirt that had Avery wondering what it would feel like to run her hands across his arm or chest.

Poppy flashed approving smiles each time they passed her staging the booth, usually laughing, since Hawthorne had that effect on her. At Poppy's unsubtle behavior, Avery realized this had all been a setup. Maybe she owed Poppy a favor, because after the pumpkins were unloaded and Poppy had everything exactly how she wanted it, she waved Avery and Hawthorne away to enjoy the festival.

They left their coats behind the table and headed toward the funnel cake truck. It was still early, and the sun combined with the work kept them warm. When Hawthorne joined his hand with hers, her temperature rose a few more degrees. They strolled through the festival, booths still in various stages of setup.

The haybale maze was complete and when Hawthorne tugged her inside, she didn't resist. Around a few corners, the sound of children playing and music from the small stage faded and they were in their own little world.

"You know," Hawthorne said, "I always wanted to make out with someone in the hayloft." At Avery's skeptical glance, he laughed. "What? It was the most private place on the farm. Do you know how hard it is to find privacy with six sisters running around?"

She didn't know, but she laughed at his flirtatious comment. "This isn't a hayloft," she said, trying to reign in her attraction.

With a shrug, he looked around. In their wandering, they'd reached a dead-end and were surrounded on three sides by hay bales six feet high. He looked back at her and Avery swore she could feel her heart hammering.

"I know." Hawthorne took a step closer, "I still think it would work, though." Avery felt like her knees would buckle any second. Hawthorne still held her hand and used it to close the space between them, wrapping his other arm around her waist. Then, he whispered, "What do you think?"

Her mind was totally blank, unable to put two words together into a coherent thought. What had he said? "Huh?"

A little smirk danced on his lips, showing he knew exactly the effect he had on her. He spoke quietly, his voice smooth and seductive. "Do you think making out in here would be roughly equivalent to in the hayloft?"

"Ummm..." She blinked, willing herself to respond. Frozen by his closeness and by the intensity of his gaze, she nodded absently, her eyes glued to his lips and the crooked smirk there.

"Let's find out," he whispered, and she might have moaned in relief. Every muscle in her body was tensed, desperately waiting for the eventual crash of his lips against hers. Finally—mercifully—he closed the gap between them and captured her mouth with his. His mouth on hers was gentle and warm, but he didn't simply kiss her. Hawthorne's kiss consumed her; she pressed into him and lost herself in the fabulous feeling of being desired.

Minutes passed, maybe hours. She couldn't tell. There was nothing beyond this secluded corner, where Hawthorne's strong frame pressed against hers and his arms cradled her gently.

Through the hazy fog of pleasure, the sound of footsteps and voices grew closer and Hawthorne broke the kiss, stepping away from her. Moments later, tiny faces sprinted into view before halting at the sight of the dead end.

With a friendly shrug, Hawthorne spoke to the

children. "Sorry! You must have missed a turn." Avery licked her lips and tried not to look guilty, flashing a smile at the children as they turned away to continue their journey through the maze.

Avery fought the self-conscious feeling that hovered. She was drawn to Hawthorne, that much was undeniable. Where did they go from here?

The rational side of her brain was screeching at her, reminding her of past mistakes. The memories of Brandon taunted her. He stood her up for dinner with her parents, which was both humiliating and disrespectful. One finals week she'd gotten sick and instead of staying with her, he ditched her to go skiing.

Any time it came to stepping up and showing he could be serious, Brandon dodged responsibility, then talked her into forgiving him with a boyish smile and puppy dog eyes.

There was nothing to reassure her Hawthorne wasn't the same. Sure, he said the right things: how he wanted to take on more responsibility at work and how he wanted a family. But talk was cheap, and Avery wasn't looking for a bargain.

Still, she couldn't help but hope his transformation was real. Did too many years of idealizing

Hawthorne have her seeing things that weren't there? Or was he really growing up?

Today though, it felt too good to ignore that logical train of thought. When Hawthorne grabbed her hand again and lead her into the maze, she followed, enjoying the feel of his skin on hers.

Today, she'd let herself enjoy the Hawthorne she was with, without thoughts of the future or the past. He'd done nothing lately to make her doubt his ability to commit. There was too much pulling her to him for her to keep pushing him away.

They enjoyed the rest of the festival, sharing a funnel cake. Avery nearly dropped the plate when Hawthorne leaned down to kiss powdered sugar from her lip. Would it always be this way with him?

When the temperature fell and they both retrieved their coats, a few teasing comments from Poppy brought nothing but a smile. Avery could tell Poppy was happy she and Hawthorne were together.

Together sounded pretty good to her, too.

12

A few weeks later, Hawthorne stopped by his mom's office inside the main house. The grungy pocket notebook he carried on the farm wasn't working for his new project management role. His mom was busy in the kitchen baking pies and cookies for Thanksgiving, only a few days away.

Thanksgiving at the Bloom home had always been a production. Hawthorne remembered the holiday being filled with cousins and extended family as a kid. Since they'd all gotten older, and many of his cousins had kids of their own, family holidays had transitioned to a big celebration with their immediate family plus whoever his mother adopted for the event.

This year, it meant seeing Avery.

A small thrill fluttered in his chest at the thought. Since the fall festival, they'd talked every couple of nights, and he'd seen her a couple times for dinner or a movie. A few nights ago, they talked on the phone for nearly two hours and, after all the twists and turns their conversation had taken, he still hadn't been ready to say goodnight. They'd texted back and forth every day, and the very feel of his phone buzzing in his pocket pulled an involuntary smile to his face.

This week, waiting until Thursday to see her seemed an incredibly long time.

He flipped through the small stockroom of office supplies his mother kept as their own personal supply store. The woman had a problem, if the fifteen unopened packages of highlighters were any indication. More pens, sticky notes, and markers than he figured the farm would use in a decade sat on the shelves in front of him.

Avery loves office supplies; hadn't she said that the other night? With an idea forming in the back of his mind, Hawthorne went to talk to his mother. When he found her, she was carefully crimping the edges of a pie crust.

At the heavy sound of his boots on the wood

floor, she looked up. "Oh, Hawthorne. I thought you were your father. Have you seen him?"

Hawthorne shook his head. "He's probably down with Rose. She said something about a school group coming today."

His mother nodded, "I assume you aren't here to help with the pies, so what brings you to the house?"

Hawthorne held up the office supplies he had pilfered from her stash and explained what he needed.

His mother gave a knowing smile, "Of course, sweetie. Help yourself to whatever you need." The timer on the stove rang through the quiet kitchen. "Would you grab those?"

Hawthorne donned an oven mitt and pulled out a baking tray to find familiar treats greeting him from behind the blast of hot air.

"Oooh, pie-crust cookies?" As soon as he set it down, he pulled one off the tray and tossed the cookie quickly between his hands. Finally, when it no longer singed his fingers, he popped the cinnamon-sugared cookie into his mouth.

Laura shook her head and he grinned around the mouthful. Unable to speak, he gave his mom a thumbs-up.

His mother let out a quiet laugh. "Honestly, I

think those are the only reason it's worth making a crust from scratch anymore. Every year, I am more and more tempted to use a store-bought one."

Hawthorne swallowed the scorching mouthful, "I promise I won't complain if you do. But I can't promise Poppy would forgive you," he said with a wink.

His mom chuckled. "I'm sure she'd understand. It's your father who would claim to understand and then silently protest." The love in his mother's voice made Hawthorne twinge with jealousy.

How would it feel to have a love like his parents did? He'd grown up running into the kitchen for a snack to find them making out. Both of them regularly put time, effort, and money into something for the sole purpose of making the other happy, like the pecan pie he knew his mother would make. She hated pecan pie, and no one else in the family ate it—except his father.

But every year, Mom would boil sugar and corn syrup and make his father an entire pie. Just like each morning, Dad would bring his mom a steaming cup of coffee to bed, even though he never drank it himself.

Cynically, Hawthorne had always thought that kind of love unattainable. His parents had found it, against all odds, but after he said as much to his mother, her response surprised him.

Laura wiped her hands on her apron, laid a hand on his shoulder and said, "A successful marriage isn't fifty-fifty. It's both people giving one hundred percent, all the time. Love is a choice, Hawthorne. At first, it's an easy choice. It's easy to love someone and the way they make you feel when it's all butterflies, but eventually it's a harder choice—when they hurt you or when their desires clash with yours." She looked into his eyes, studying his expression. "Do you love her?"

Afraid his mom would see too much in them, Hawthorne closed his eyes and shook his head. "I don't know. It's still butterflies," he admitted.

He opened his eyes to find his mom with a knowing smiling. She turned back to the counter and dumped pecans into the pie shell cooling on the rack. "Well, then enjoy it." She gestured to the office supplies with an empty measuring spoon, "I hope she likes them."

Hawthorne grinned, "Me too."

That afternoon, he drove to Terre Haute and found a parking spot on campus. It had been more than ten years since he'd stepped foot on university grounds, but he still remembered the rundown

Chemistry building where he'd suffered through basic chem lab on his way to a business degree. The halls were a ghost-town, an empty shell with flyers stapled to bulletin boards that fluttered in the breeze as he opened the door. His footsteps echoed loudly as he glanced at nameplates, awkwardly holding his gift. Finally, Hawthorne found a secretary and she directed him to Avery's office, tucked in a hidden corner of the basement.

He peeked his head in the room, dismayed to find her chair empty. Briefly, he debated his options and finally settled on leaving the makeshift bouquet of office supplies on her desk. Hawthorne jotted a note in the first page of a bound notebook and propped it open so she would see it. The ragged chair groaned as he stood and Hawthorne once more studied the space. There were no windows and flickering fluorescent lights cast a depressing pallor, but touches of Avery dotted the room: a framed photo of her family, and science-themed cartoons. Sticky notes lined the monitor with reminders and email addresses in her loopy script.

You couldn't pay him enough to work in this cave. Even the modern, airy offices of his own start-up left him feeling claustrophobic after a few hours. Glass walls didn't compare to the wide-open spaces of the farm, and something about miles of sky above him allowed his soul to take a deep breath. Coming back to the farm relieved the subtle tension that stretched him thin while he was away.

With one last glance around the empty office, Hawthorne backtracked through the maze of hallways to his car, pushing down the disappointment of not seeing Avery. He would see her Thursday at Thanksgiving, and hopefully his little surprise would brighten her day.

Avery set the last beaker in the drying rack and wiped her hands on a towel with a sigh. Her undergraduate assistant had skipped out early from work last night, leaving the glassware from their last experiment a mess of dried deposits. Thankfully, it was not an acid that became combustible when dry, but it was still a safety hazard and would mean a restriction on lab access for the student moving forward.

She left the lab and headed back to her office. Edward exited the copy room just as she walked past, and Avery forced a smile. Despite his office being on the opposite side of the building, he insisted on walking her to hers. Edward followed her into the small room and she gritted her teeth, biting back the unkind words itching to come out.

"Oh, what's this?" she heard his curiosity and rolled her eyes as she finished hanging her lab coat on the back of the door. He'd been in her office a dozen times and this manufactured excuse to prolong the conversation was too obvious. Why hadn't he gotten the point after their date?

"Edward-" she said as she turned. Then, she spotted the object of his curiosity. Edward leaned over her desk, peering through his glasses with his hands behind his back. Avery plucked the open notebook from his view and glanced at the signature. Hawthorne had been here? Another wave of frustration at the research assistant washed over her.

"Someone left you school supplies?" Edward's distaste was evident in the question.

Avery blushed. "My b-boyfriend," she stuttered. Then, with added confidence, "I must have missed his visit."

Edward voice cracked, "Boyfriend?" Avery nodded and then pushed her way around Edward to take her seat.

He lifted his chin, "Shouldn't a man bring a lady flowers?"

One finger traced the ribbon of the notebook

while she studied the bouquet and Avery glanced at Edward, "I suppose it depends on the girl." In total dismissal, she picked up the receiver of her office phone and looked away from her unwanted guest. "Thanks for stopping by, Edward. I need to call my *boyfriend* and tell him thank you."

After he left, Avery set down the phone, realizing she didn't actually know his phone number by heart. Either way, she wanted to enjoy the gift for a moment before she called him. Running a hand over the sticky notes, highlighters, and markers that were creatively attached to stiff metal wires, she flipped open the notebook and read the words he'd written.

After a moment, her eyes moved back to the start and read it again.

Then, she leaned back and tipped the open notebook toward her chest with a dreamy sigh. The man was good, she had to admit. Had she ever received a gift so clearly designed for her, for no other reason than he was thinking of her? Footsteps echoed outside her door and Avery realized she was smiling like an idiot at her desk. Unable to wipe the smile away, she buried her face in the notebook and laughed.

Avery felt special and inexplicably understood by Hawthorne. A dangerous combination when added to the physical pull she felt whenever she was near him, and the admiration and respect growing for him every day. Avery didn't know what to do; every fiber of her being was drawn to Hawthorne. She found herself looking for any excuse she could find to visit the farm, and the text messages they'd exchanged all weekend had her turning on cheesy songs from her childhood and dancing through her apartment while cleaning.

13

*A*very had to wait until she left work to reach out to Hawthorne; her basement cave was a total black hole for cell reception. When she called, Hawthorne picked up immediately. Uncertainty and relief filled his voice after she told him how much she enjoyed the gift.

Upon hearing that Edward had been with her when she found it, Hawthorne gave a jealous grunt and the sound vibrated within her, spreading warmth from the base of her stomach up to her ears. She admitted telling Edward her boyfriend had sent them, and she practically felt Hawthorne's satisfied smile through the phone.

Hawthorne invited her to come to the farm in the morning before Thanksgiving dinner. He assured her they wouldn't be in his mom's way, so she pulled her car in front of his house at 9 a.m. The sight of Hawthorne jogging down the steps in a stocking cap, his shaggy brown hair flipping out under the edges, broadened the already wide smile she wore. He opened her car door and, after she stepped out, wrapped her in a hug that overwhelmed her senses.

Hawthorne murmured in her ear, "I missed you," before capturing her lips in a kiss. Breaking the kiss, he picked her up and spun her around. The flying sensation in her belly was due to more than the spinning and Avery let out a joyful laugh.

With her feet firmly on the ground again, Avery said, "Well, good morning to you, too."

Hawthorne gave a sheepish smile, "Sorry. It's just good to see you."

Shaking her head, Avery replied, "No, it's perfect."

Hawthorne had been up since before six helping his sisters with the chores that needed done. He must have already showered though, since Avery only detected the lemon soap and the faintest hint of the barn on his coat.

The sun was shining and although the air was brisk, the usual biting wind was still this morning.

Gloved hand in gloved hand, they walked from the old homestead to the barn, about a ten-minute walk. A vehicle approached from the other direction and Avery considered pulling her hand from Hawthorne's, but he gave her hand a quick squeeze. The simple action settled her nerves, and as Poppy drove past in the UTV with a friendly wave, Avery responded with one of her own.

Hawthorne saddled horses for them and with a brief hello to Rose, the two of them took off along the fence line. As a kid on the farm, they hadn't been allowed to ride the horses alone, and Avery had only explored the property from the seat of a UTV. They were mostly for work and she remembered the stern lecture they'd all received when Keith caught the girls joyriding across the pasture.

There was something different about seeing it from horseback though. She said as much to Hawthorne, and he smiled in understanding. Releasing the reins, he spread his arms and waved to the wide-open sky. He let out a loud yell into the space and his horse started, causing Hawthorne to wobble and lower his arms to catch his balance on the saddle horn. He laughed, and once Avery's heart recovered from its missed beats, she was able to shake her head in amusement.

"Doesn't it just make you feel insignificant?" he mused.

Avery looked, finding the horizon across the plains. A formation of geese crossed their view in a lopsided V. She nodded, "It does, but it also makes me think of how Jesus said God feeds the birds of the air and how much more He cares for us. It's humbling to realize how small we are but yet, how much God loves us." Afraid to look at the man next to her, she spoke to the pasture instead. They'd touched on other deep subjects over the phone, but she hadn't spoken so openly about her faith to Hawthorne yet.

Hawthorne sat silently, the padded fall of hooves on grassy dirt the only sound. Then he spoke, "I was reading a psalm this morning that talked about how God created everything and then put man over it all. The birds, the fields, the whole earth. All of it was created by God and then given to us to care for. It's incredible."

Avery felt love for Hawthorne bubble over inside her as she listened to him speak of their Creator. Until now, it had been simmering and slowly building—waiting for permission to crest into something she could truly embrace. The gentle rocking of Avery's horse seemed too slow, too tame compared to the pure, unadulterated joy she felt when she watched Hawthorne study the land, poised tall on the horse next to her. He was honorable, thoughtful, and kind. She'd seen how he cared for his family and heard him speak of the plans and love for the farm. He was steady and strong. And, oh, she loved him!

"Want to race?" The boyish grin crossed Hawthorne's face, replacing the contemplative look she'd seen there moments before.

Instead of answering, Avery nudged Cappuccino with her heels and lowered herself toward the horse's mane. It wasn't long before she heard the thunder of hooves behind her as Hawthorne gained ground. Kicking again, she urged Cappuccino faster as the wind whipped through her hair and stung her chilled nose. A glance back revealed the grinning face of Hawthorne pursuing her, just as he had since he walked back into her life.

Slowing to a trot and then a walk, they ended their horseback ride back at the barn and brushed down the horses. Hawthorne pulled apples from a bag on the wall along with a scoop of oats for each animal. Avery was petting her horse on the nose until Hawthorne turned to her and grabbed her hand. Pulling her close to him, he wrapped his hands around Avery's waist and looked down at her.

"Thanks for coming over early. I wasn't ready to share you with my family quite yet."

Avery felt a blush, despite the stiffness of her cheeks, still frozen from their time outside. "About that..." She struggled for the words to ask what she needed to. "What do we tell your family?"

Hawthorne gave her an amused smile. "I was thinking about telling them that I'm in love with you."

Avery felt her mouth fall open, her eyes wide in shock.

"Don't look so surprised, beautiful. Surely, you knew that's where we were headed?"

Avery closed her eyes to fight the tears. She nodded, "I did. But—"

"No buts. Let's go see what's going on at the house." Hawthorne released her and tugged her hand toward the exit.

Avery's feet were cemented to the floor, though, and she found herself unable to follow. She wasn't done having this conversation, and she wasn't about to let him walk away without hearing what she had to say.

"Wait," she tugged on his hand. "You didn't let me say anything."

Hawthorn raised an eyebrow at her. "Okay, go for it."

Avery swallowed, "You love me?"

He chuckled and stepped in close to meet her gaze. Grabbing her hands and rubbing them with his own, he spoke softly, "Avery Gabrielle Chase, I love you. Desperately," he added. Then he looked back down at their joined hands.

Avery nodded. "Good. Because I love you, too."

Hawthorne's movements froze and he looked up sharply. "What did you say?"

"Surely, you knew that's where we were headed?" she teased. She squeezed his hands and flashed a smile.

Dropping her hands, strong arms wrapped around her as he spun them around with a loud cheer. When her feet finally found the ground again, he pulled off her stocking cap and reached behind her neck with one hand to pull her in for a breath-stealing kiss. Happy to get lost in the moment, she melted into him, focusing entirely on the feel of her lips on his and the warmth of his arms around her.

The sound of someone clearing their throat broke the spell and Avery buried her face in Hawthorne's shoulder, afraid to see which member of his family had caught them. Hawthorne's voice rumbled in his chest against her cheek as he spoke. "Hey, Dad. What's up?"

First Miss Laura in the hallway and now his dad? Avery stepped back and smiled shyly.

"Hey, son. Avery. Good to see you." A small smile twitched on Keith's face, but was gone in an instant. "Just thought I heard..." He trailed off, looking around in confusion.

"Are you looking for Rose?" Hawthorne asked.

Keith took a few steps, looking behind him and then into the horse stall with a bewildered look on his face. "What? I'm look...unngh." The words began to sound heavy and slurred, he tried again. "Whaaramm?" he mumbled and one eye drooped closed, his tongue lolling to one side.

Avery looked on in horror as Keith wobbled, falling to the side and crashing into the doorframe as one leg buckled under him. She felt the cold race to fill the empty space beside her as Hawthorne suddenly released her and rushed to his father's side.

Garbled syllables were all that emerged when Keith tried to speak and Avery had a flash of recognition. "A stroke. He's having a stroke," she said, her voice firm and urgent.

Hawthorne looked up at her with a fierce look. "Get help," he ordered.

Avery took one last glance at the strong man, crumpled in a heap on the barn floor, then stumbled outside. Numb fingers retrieved her cell phone and managed to punch in Daisy's number. No answer. With a desperate prayer, Avery called 911 as she hopped on the four-wheeler.

---

*H*awthorne rested his head in his hands, then ran them through his hair for the thousandth time before sitting back up. The quiet drone of the Thanksgiving Parade coverage filled the otherwise silent waiting room. He watched his mother hug her upper arms and pace the small room, muttering to herself. Praying?

After the adrenaline rush of watching his father collapse before his eyes, Hawthorne couldn't do anything. Even a simple prayer felt like a monumental task he didn't have the energy to tackle.

A stroke, Avery had said. The minutes from when she walked out to when his mom and sisters arrived at the barn felt like hours. Hawthorne had never felt so helpless as he did watching his father struggle, confused and unable to stand or speak. For endless minutes, he'd listened to his father try to form words without success. Hawthorne attempted to settle and reassure him, but his father's limp hand in his own had been disconcerting, and, unsure of what to do, Hawthorne had covered his father with a nearby horse blanket and waited.

His family arrived and the paramedics came shortly after. Now, they all sat in the bleak waiting room. He hadn't seen or heard from Avery since she'd run out of the barn, a look of determination on her face. His phone was still back at his house.

A doctor stepped into the waiting area and found his mother, so Hawthorne stepped close and put his arm around her. She felt small and frail as she leaned into him.

The doctor was kind but matter of fact in his explanation, "Mrs. Bloom, your husband had an ischemic stroke." Hawthorne felt his throat go dry. "We did a CT scan upon arrival to rule out hemorrhaging and have started a drug that will target the clot and break it up. We won't know what the lasting impact is until a few days have passed."

His mom clutched Hawthorne's arm and asked, "Can we see him?"

The doctor nodded, "One at a time for now."

Hawthorne squeezed his mother's hand and motioned for her to go. His sisters were all waiting, anxiously standing next to their chairs on the other side of the room; he would tell them what the doctor said. Pinched, worried faces stared back at him as he approached.

"Well?" Lavender spoke timidly, her arm around Rose and fresh tear tracks still wet on her face.

He looked at his sisters and relayed the message from the doctor. "Now, we wait."

"We need to call Andi," Daisy said.

Hawthorne nodded, "That's a good idea." He glanced at his watch and said, "It's nearly 9 p.m. there, maybe you can catch her before she turns in."

Daisy shuffled out of the room with her phone in hand, reminding Hawthorne again that his own was back home. He felt a tap on his shoulder and when he turned, Poppy placed her phone in his hand, Avery's contact info already pulled up on the screen. Taking it, he sent his sister a grateful glance and followed Daisy out of the room as Lily gathered the remaining group.

"Come here, Rose, Lavender. Prayer is the best thing we can do. Poppy, why don't you start?" Lily's calm voice faded away as the he turned the corner.

Avery's voice met his ears, "Poppy? Is everything

okay?" Hawthorne sagged against the cold concrete pillar at the sound.

"It's me," he said, his voice thick with unexpected emotion.

Relief filled her voice, "Hawthorne, how is he?"

After relaying the doctor's words, Hawthorne paused. "Are you okay?"

"Me? I'm fine," Avery sounded confused, but understanding filled her voice when she continued softly, "Are you?"

"I don't know, Aves. I—" his voice broke, "I've never seen him like that before, you know?" His dad had been so helpless. As long as he could remember, his dad was a giant, loud and full of life. Memories of playing catch or riding around on his shoulders disintegrated into the vision of his dad, ashen and weak on the floor. "What am I supposed to do without him?" Then, the gravity of the potential future hit him, "What is our family supposed to do?" Dad had always been the foundation on which everything was built. Without Keith Bloom, what would become of Bloom's Farm?

Avery spoke quickly, her voice soothing and reassuring. But instead of providing comfort, her words sent his heart racing and his head swimming. "It's going to be okay. You and your sisters are more than capable of running the farm. Your mom needs you to be strong and so do your sisters. You can do this, Hawthorne. I believe in you."

They needed him? That was the terrifying part. Sure, Avery believed in him, but did he believe in himself? People had needed him to be a leader before and he'd ruined their lives and wrecked his business. What was to say he wouldn't do the same thing to Bloom's Farm given the chance?

Avery was still talking, "I'll keep praying for your Dad, okay? He might be totally fine!" Hawthorne made a few noncommittal noises and ended the call, sinking onto the bench in the main hospital atrium. He wasn't ready for this. If his dad wasn't okay, Hawthorne couldn't be the one to take on more control. Wouldn't.

He wasn't ready. Only two months ago, he'd been out every night with his friends and actively avoiding additional responsibility on the farm. Hawthorne felt the acid rise in his throat, his stomach cramping in refusal at the thought of taking charge. It had been awful when the company he built had collapsed, his friends out of work and his own time and energy all for naught. Visions of Bloom's Farm with a giant For Sale sign and his sisters packing their belongings into cardboard boxes harassed him when he closed his eyes and leaned his head back against the cold, concrete pillar. However irrational it seemed, Hawthorne couldn't shake the certainty that if he were in charge of Bloom's Farm, it would go under.

It had to be Poppy. Or Lily. Both were more than capable, already managing their own branch of the farm with ease. He, on the other hand, had only stepped beyond his role as handyman a month ago. Who was he kidding? If the panicky feeling in his chest was any indication, he was nowhere near equipped to handle the responsibility of managing the farm. No way.

Avery put away all the food Laura left behind in the chaos, wrapping untouched stuffing and pies in foil and storing potatoes and green bean casserole in plastic containers. She let the turkey finish cooking, then pulled it out and carved it into slices before packing it away as well. After she heard from Hawthorne and finally admitted no one was coming back here anytime soon, she wiped down the counters and cleared the table.

To fill the eerie silence, and because it was the

best thing to do, Avery prayed—not only for Keith's health, but for Laura and each of the Bloom siblings. Especially Hawthorne. She couldn't put her finger on it, but he hadn't sounded like himself when they'd talked. Chalking it up to the stress of the day and fatigue or worry, she tried to push away her own concerns. But the nagging feeling that something wasn't right with Hawthorne continued to eat at her, and she repeated her prayers again and again.

When there was nothing left to do in a kitchen that didn't belong to her, Avery flipped off the lights and locked the door behind her. She walked back to the old homestead, bracing herself against the wind that had picked up as the day grew older and the sun started to sink down.

She called her sister on her way home. "Hey Brie," she said with little enthusiasm.

"Avery! Happy Thanksgiving! Just a second, let me get Mom and Dad!" Her sister's carefree voice sang through the receiver, discordant against the heavy anxiety of Avery's own mood.

Soon, she heard a chorus of hellos from her parents. They chattered excitedly about the snow and the tree lighting ceremony coming up on Sunday. The tourist town of Freedom, Colorado embraced Christmas with wide open arms, and ski season was in full swing.

"How was dinner with the Bloom's?" her mother asked.

Avery started to tear up as she recounted the day's events. "It was awful. I just feel terrible for their whole family."

"Oh dear, I'm so sorry. Poor Laura," her mother exclaimed, "We'll need to send flowers, okay Drew?"

"Sounds good, dear," her father replied, almost automatically.

Avery smiled at the familiar lilt of their conversation. She pulled into her apartment parking lot and started to say goodbye. "I just wanted to let you know I'm thankful for all of you, and I miss you." She squeezed the steering wheel and pressed her eyes closed against the threat of tears.

"We miss you, too! Come visit us again soon, okay?"

The burning in her throat made it difficult to respond, but she choked out an acknowledgment and hung up the phone. Today had been a rollercoaster of emotions, from the joyous laughter of the horseback ride to the tender thrill of declarations of love. Followed, of course, by the unparalleled shock and fear of watching Keith Bloom transform from perfectly normal to a confused shell, robbed of speech. Then to the loneliness of being the only one left behind when the family followed the ambulance to the hospital.

Not that she expected to be remembered in the chaos. Nevertheless, it was disconcerting to walk into the kitchen bustling with activity and have it completely cleared with a handful of words. Lily, ever the responsible one, had stayed behind trying to turn off the stove and burners before Avery had waved her out. She still felt her small contribution was a tangible way to show love and help the family while they navigated this crisis. But oh, how she'd much rather be there in the waiting room with Hawthorne, letting him lean on her. They were a team now, right?

She'd sent him several messages throughout the day, but his calling from Poppy's phone was a pretty good indication that he didn't have his own. Which didn't stop her from checking for a message notification every thirty seconds.

Avery dropped her bag next to the door and kicked one boot off in the entryway, the other a few steps later. Collapsing on the couch, unable to even complete the few steps further into the bedroom, she immediately fell asleep, still in her coat.

Hours later, the sound of ringing and buzzing pierced the silence and she opened her eyes groggily. She reached frantically for the phone, knocking it off the coffee table and fumbling for it on the woven rug. Poppy's name flashed on the screen before it went dark. One missed call.

Quickly, she called back, and surprise filled her when Poppy's voice greeted her instead of Hawthorne's.

"Hey, Avery." Poppy sounded so tired, and Avery's heart went out to her friend.

"How's it going?"

Poppy had no update on her dad, but her next words dropped a curtain of cold over Avery, despite the coat she still wore, "Is Hawthorne with you?"

Avery sat up straight, looking around her small living room for the face she knew wasn't there. "What? No. He's still at the hospital, isn't he?"

15

*H*awthorne stared at the video game controller in his hands and listened to Shayne swear at the character he'd just blown up. He hadn't seen Shayne and Craig since the night Avery had scolded them at the bar. He hadn't really missed them, but when the thought of walking into his dad's hospital room had been too much to handle, he'd left without a word to his sisters and caught a cab to Shayne's apartment.

It was just a bad coincidence that he happened to live in the same giant apartment complex as Avery. She was only four buildings away — close enough to walk, even in the cold night. She didn't know he was a coward yet, and he pictured her warm smile when she saw him at her door. The physical relief he knew would come at her very presence called to him, a siren from around the corner.

Avery would find out eventually that he wasn't the man she hoped he was. He'd almost fooled himself into thinking he could be the guy with a wife and work responsibilities. Almost. Until the reality of taking over was staring him in the face, struggling to speak and looking at him with confused eyes and a slack jaw.

"Boom! That's what I'm talking about!" Shayne exclaimed.

Hawthorne sighed and punched the button to respawn his character. Trying to pull his focus away from his own impossible situation, he tried to talk to Shayne. "No plans for Thanksgiving?"

Shayne twisted the controller and his body, trying to force his on-screen character to dodge a piece of shrapnel. "What? Oh, my mom had the whole family over—my weird uncles and everything. I grabbed lunch and then bailed on those losers." Shayne's cruel laugh grated Hawthorne's nerves.

How was he friends with someone so ungrateful and selfish? Shayne hadn't even asked why Hawthorne was there or why he hadn't been around lately. Why did he come here? He could have gone to Josh's. Or Avery's.

Again, the urge to walk to her place was over-whelming, but his insecurities chained him to the couch. Both Josh and Avery would never let him get away with his current behavior. Oh, they'd go about it in different ways—he could already picture Josh's raised eyebrow and incredulous, "Really, dude?"

And Avery? She'd either punch him on the shoulder or give him an icy glare. Or the same look of disappointment she'd given him at the bar. It would be a thousand times worse now, knowing how it felt to have her look at him with admiration and love. She loved him, or at least the man he'd been impersonat-ing. Avery loved the idea of a Hawthorne who was responsible and trustworthy and could handle the blows of life. He wasn't that man.

It was so much easier to hang out here, killing zombies with someone holding no expectations of him—or themselves, for that matter. Even if that someone seemed more immature and irritating by the minute.

Shayne yelled in celebration as he hit the last target and set down his controller. Heading to the kitchen, he casually asked Hawthorne if he wanted another drink.

Did he? It would be easy to have another. He could sleep here all night and drown his own unhappiness and self-doubt in the bottom of a bottle and meaningless conversation. That's what he had done most nights since his company went under. Until a month ago. Until Avery.

He'd been happier in the last month than he had in years, and he realized it didn't all have to do with Avery. That was part of it, definitely. He'd made other changes, though. It seemed like weeks had passed, but what he'd said to Avery this afternoon was true—he'd been reading his Bible. His faith had been strong once upon a time, and the wake-up call Avery gave him that night in the bar was the push he needed.

He'd been sleeping better, praying more. He'd been happier and more grateful. Patient with his sisters. All because he'd ditched his loser friends and started focusing on Jesus? It seemed too easy.

And spending time with Avery. Was it cliché to say she made him want to be a better man? Maybe. But it didn't mean it wasn't true. Had he really ever thought these superficial conversations and wasted time were fun?

Shayne handed him a bottle and after opening the cap on his own, tossed Hawthorne the bottle opener. Hawthorne positioned the opener against the top but held it there, unwilling to apply the slight pressure that would bend the metal bottle cap just enough to break the seal.

He set the bottle and the opener down on the coffee table, next to the controller he'd been using. "I gotta run, man. Thanks for letting me hide out here for a bit."

Bathed in the glow of flickering blue light, Shayne waved a hand but didn't look away from the screen, already completely engrossed in his game. Hawthorne slipped his shoes on and zipped up his jacket. He needed to see someone who cared.

Ten minutes later, he rapped a knuckle on Avery's apartment door. The neighbor's light flicked on and Hawthorne had the sudden realization that he had no idea what time it was. He'd never gone back to the farm to get his phone, and he'd been at Shayne's at least long enough for them to order pizza and beat three or four levels in the game. Was it 8 o'clock? Maybe 9?

He knocked again. *Please let her open the door,* he prayed.

Finally, the door opened and he felt the tension drain from his body at the sight of Avery's sleep-laden eyes and rumpled hair. She wore loose pajama pants covered in beakers and electron diagrams, and tightened a sweater around her shoulders before opening the door wider and gesturing him in wordlessly.

He stepped out of his shoes and followed her as she ambled ahead of him to turn into the kitchen.

"Coffee?" she asked, already filling up the coffee pot.

"Coffee sounds great." Hawthorne watched the woman he loved scoop coffee into the filter and retrieve mugs from the cabinet, stretching on her bare tiptoes to reach the shelf.

"My dad—" Hawthorne started to speak, but Avery held up a hand.

"Coffee first." She glanced at the clock, "It's midnight."

Hawthorne followed her gaze and read the green numbers for himself. How was that even possible?

"I'm sorry, Aves. I'll go and come back another time."

Avery shook her head. "Not a chance. Go sit down." She pulled creamer from the fridge before turning back to him. "My phone is on the table. Text your sisters and let them know you're okay. They've been worried sick."

Hawthorne felt the heavy weight settle in the pit of his stomach this time. His sisters. He winced. "I'm the worst—" he started, but once again was interrupted.

"Go. Tell your family you are okay." Hawthorne nodded his agreement. Avery was right; the self-pity could wait. For now, he had to start making the right choice. Coming here was the first one, reassuring his family was the next. After that? He still wasn't sure.

Standing in the hospital with his mother and letting her lean on him had seemed natural. Stepping up on the farm and contributing ideas was becoming easier every day. Taking control and coordinating the caravan from the farm to the hospital had been instinctual in a moment of chaos.

But the thought of running the farm? Filling his father's shoes seemed impossible, like he'd be a toddler playing dress-up, destined to fall flat on his face after one step.

16

*A*very put both hands on the kitchen counter and released a heavy breath. What was Hawthorne thinking? Since Poppy called around eight o'clock, Avery had swung back and forth from worry to anger to understanding and back again. She'd continued to pray fervently for Hawthorne until she finally drifted back to sleep. It was amazing how emotional marathons were just as exhausting as actual workouts. Hence, the coffee being brewed before her still-blurry eyes.

Coffee first, then glasses.

As soon as there was enough coffee in the pot for two mugs, Avery interrupted the brewing process, added cream, and carried the drinks to the living room. Hawthorne sat on the couch, his elbows resting on his knees and his hands clasped together under his forehead.

Sliding a coaster closer to him, she set his coffee on it and then carried her own to her bathroom. With her glasses on, Avery could clearly see the smudged makeup she'd never washed off, the blotchy cheeks from tears she'd cried, and the messy bun that had officially crossed over from casually cute to definitely disastrous. She settled for a quick swipe of makeup remover under her eyes and a hurried repositioning of the ponytail. Good enough for midnight.

Hawthorne didn't appear to have moved a muscle and she settled soundlessly onto the arm chair across the room from him. In the silence of the apartment, though, he heard her and looked up. A smile flickered across his face.

"I'm sorry, Avery," he said, breaking the peaceful stillness of the room.

A tortured expression haunted his features and her heart broke for him. If she felt like she'd run a marathon, he must feel like he'd been run over and tied in knots by a hay baler.

"Tell me what happened," Avery responded.

Hawthorne grabbed his coffee, still leaning over his knees and perched on the edge of the sofa. "We got to the hospital and there was nothing we could do except wait. I told the paramedics exactly what we saw. How dad was—" his voice broke "—how he was perfectly fine until he just... wasn't."

Staring into the black well of his mug, Hawthorne continued, "Mom gripped my arm so hard she left bruises when the doctor came out."

"I can't imagine what she must be feeling," Avery said absently.

Hawthorne leaned back and shook his head, looking at Avery. "I'm starting to, I think. The idea of losing the person who makes you feel whole? It's terrifying."

Avery's heart fluttered, but they hadn't covered the important part yet.

"What happened next? Why did you disappear?" She kept hoping she would hear him say how he went back to the farm to care for animals. Or that he went to a church to pray. Somehow, she knew that wouldn't be the explanation.

"I called a cab from the hospital and went to Shayne's."

Avery recoiled. "You skipped out on your family at the hospital and refused to see your father after his stroke to go visit Shayne?"

Hawthorne set his untouched coffee back on the

table. "I know, it was stupid. I just needed to not think for a while. I needed to go somewhere with no expectations." He ran his hands over his cheeks and chin. "You were talking about how my mom and my sisters need me. How I could step up and run the farm for my dad until he is better. *If* he gets better," he said with anguish. Then, his voice full of self-loathing, "I just panicked."

Indignation rose in her throat and Avery tried to push it down and find sympathy without success. Skepticism filled her voice instead as she responded, "And now?"

Hawthorne glanced at her. "Honestly? I'm still panicking. But I realized I needed to be with someone who cared and who makes me want to be better. That isn't Shayne and the mindless video games." He slid from the couch and made his way in front of her chair, laying his hand on her knee and his back against the chair leg. "I needed to be with you. I don't know how to navigate this, Avery. I need you and I need God, but it took me a while to realize it."

With his admission, Avery felt the deep wave of sympathy and love pull her under. This man, the man she loved, was hurting and she hurt with him. This vulnerability was new. The confident, charming boy she'd idealized fifteen years ago was in pieces on the floor in front of her. The warm, intelligent, strong man she'd professed to loving fifteen hours ago had been beaten down by the day.

He needed her. For years, she'd been seeking stability—looking for someone she could lean on. And now, Hawthorne needed to lean on her. Did that mean he wasn't the anchor she needed?

Maybe she had confused Brandon's selfishness for instability. She had never been able to rely on Brandon, that was true. But really, it hadn't been that he was irresponsible. It had been selfishness, pure and simple.

Could she depend on Hawthorne? Her heart leapt with the answer. If the tables were turned and she needed Hawthorne—he would be there, no questions asked. There was no doubt in her mind. Stability wasn't the same as independence. What they really needed was dependence on each other and on God. A cord of three strands.

Avery ran a hand through his impossibly soft brown hair, massaging his scalp absently, and he leaned his head into her. "I'm here, Hawthorne, but you shouldn't be."

Silky strands of hair fell through her fingers as he turned with a confused and hurt look.

Avery smiled kindly, "You need to be with your family, Hawthorne. They need you."

Hawthorne closed his eyes. "But," he whispered, "I need you."

Reveling in the warmth of his shoulder against her leg and his heart so wide open to her, she placed a kiss on the crown of his head. "You have me, but for now, your family comes first. Be the man I fell in love with. Step up and be the leader I know you are. You won't fail."

Her faith in him was humbling. "I'm afraid I can't fill his shoes," he admitted.

"I think you'll be surprised how well they fit," Avery responded after a moment. He smiled at her continuation of the analogy.

"Will you pray with me?" he asked. He'd been working on his own faith over the past weeks, uncovering a foundation he'd nearly forgotten. Today had tested him and he'd wavered, but he wasn't giving up. As much as he needed Avery, he knew he needed God more. God's strength wouldn't fail.

Still, as they prayed, Hawthorne realized that being with Avery and knowing she stood behind him was exactly what he needed. Something about love made it possible to stand in the face of opposition, imagined or not. For the first time in hours, his heart lightened, and he began to see more than the despair of the situation.

They finished praying, and he shifted gears. Hawthorne allowed the thoughts he'd pushed away all day to flood his mind. Plans started to take shape about what needed done at the farm, and who could do each critical task.

If he was going to do this, he needed a notebook. He asked, and Avery pointed at one on the coffee table. He spent fifteen minutes pouring out his thoughts, while Avery curled up behind him sipping her coffee. After the deluge of concerns was laid out on paper, he leaned back again against her flannel-clad legs.

"Thank you, Avery," he said quietly. "I love you."

She smiled behind her empty mug and set it down. "I love you, too. But now, you have to go before my neighbors get the wrong idea about this midnight visit." She nudged him forward with her leg.

Hawthorne laughed softly. "Fine. I'll go." He stood and grabbed her hand to pull her up to him.

"How did I get so lucky?" he asked before kissing her.

She pulled away with a laugh, "Thank your sisters. Somewhere along the way, it's probably all their fault. Or your mom, who invited me over. Repeatedly," she added.

He kissed her again before responding, "Mmm, I'll be sure to do that."

Another kiss and she pushed him away. "Okay, seriously, you have to go." Needing a shield, she reached back for her coffee.

"There's just one little problem," he said with an embarrassed smile. "I walked here from Shayne's and I don't have a car."

17

*A*fter Avery dropped him off at the farm, Hawthorne went upstairs and found his phone. Ignoring the thirty-nine notifications from text messages and missed calls, he sent a text message to his sisters calling a family meeting the next morning.

Main house, 9 a.m.

It was nearly two in the morning, he didn't expect anyone to answer. But it would seem trouble sleeping was an epidemic tonight, because replies kept buzzing in.

I'll be there after I feed the animals.

That was Rose, the animals always came first. Replies from Poppy and Lily chimed in minutes later.

I'll make breakfast for everyone.

Glad you came to your senses.

Then, he heard Daisy knock lightly on his bedroom door before it opened a crack.

"Come on in," he said, looking up from the notebook he'd commandeered from Avery's apartment.

Daisy walked across the room and hugged his shoulders and neck before folding herself into a sitting position on the bed where he could see her from his desk chair.

"You okay?" she asked.

He nodded, "Yeah. Better late than never, but I'm good."

"Good. I didn't know..." she swallowed and released a breath, "I didn't know what to expect when I heard you come in this late."

Hawthorne's shoulders sagged and he rolled his chair closer to the bed. "I'm sorry I haven't been a great brother. You should never have had to worry about me. And I promise that life is behind me. I was doing some soul-searching tonight. But I didn't need to look in a bar."

Daisy leaned forward and hugged him again. "Today was awful. I'm glad you are here now."

"Me too, Daze." He hugged his sister tightly.

The next morning, Hawthorne stopped by the barn and helped Rose with the animals. She greeted him wordlessly, tossing him a small rectangular bale of hay and pointing to the goat pen. A grunt at the impact of the hay bale escaped and he shook his head. Rose never pulled punches, and she had every right to be angry with him. She thawed as they worked, and by the end, she pulled him in for a hug. Rose was his youngest sister, still fresh out of college. Sometimes he still felt like she should be the baby he remembered holding when he was ten years old. Here she was, up before dawn and single-handedly managing the pigs, goats, chickens, and horses. How could she be twenty-three and more ready for responsibility than he was at thirty-three?

Together, they took the side-by-side up to the new house. Pages of notes from the night before were folded and firmly tucked in the back pocket of his jeans. Hawthorne couldn't help but finger them every so often to reassure himself they were there.

He and Rose were early for breakfast, but Poppy was in the kitchen and the second pot of coffee was already brewing. Lavender was there too, setting the table with orange juice and syrup for the pancakes.

Poppy set down the spatula and walked toward

him. With one pointy finger pressing into the tender flesh between his shoulder and collarbone, her irritation flashed. "Don't you ever pull a stunt like that again, okay?" Hawthorne bit back a laugh at his pint-sized sister's ire. Poppy made up for her size with her feisty spirit.

He held up two hands in surrender. "I promise. Scout's honor!"

Poppy narrowed her eyes at him, but must have seen his sincerity, because she removed her finger and wrapped her arms around his waist. "We were worried about you, big dummy."

"I really am sorry." He looked around at the room full of his sisters, each unique in their own way. "To all of you. I'm sorry." Lily was pouring a cup of coffee and he caught her eye. "I'm sorry, Lil." In response, she raised her mug in salute.

"Okay, I've got Andi on the line!" Daisy leaned up from the computer and her twin sister's face filled the screen, wearing sand-colored fatigues.

Andi's voice crackled from the small laptop speaker, "I've only got about fifteen minutes, guys. Give me an update on Dad."

Hawthorne looked to Lily, realizing he hadn't heard anything recently either.

"Mom's still at the hospital; she wouldn't come home last night. So far, the stroke symptoms haven't gotten any worse, which is a good sign. But they haven't gotten significantly better either, and the doctors say it's too soon to tell." Lily told Andi more about their dad's condition and what they had seen when visiting him the night before.

Andi's voice skipped as the connection buffered. "I wish I could be there with you all. I should be home for two weeks at Christmas."

Lavender piped up, "That's only four weeks away, Andi. We'll see you soon!"

Andi smiled and said, "I can't wait." Turning behind her, she waved to someone off screen, "I've got to run. We're moving out tomorrow and I've got work to do. Keep me posted."

A chorus of farewells echoed as the screen went blank and Andi's face disappeared. In the silence, Hawthorne pulled out his notes. He looked around at his sisters, all looking to him for the next steps.

He felt like a deer, frozen in the headlights and grabbed the first lifeline he could think of. "Let's all grab food and I'll talk while we eat."

He filled his own plate last but didn't take a bite.

"I want to apologize again for yesterday."

Hawthorne explained how seeing their father have his stroke had impacted him, especially in light of the changes he had been making lately.

"A little over a month ago, I talked to Mom and Dad about taking on more responsibility at the farm." His sisters, ever supportive, flashed smiles and cheered. "But when I was in the hospital looking at the very real possibility that Dad might never be the same again, I started to panic. There is still part of me that is running from this because I might fail." Quietly, he added, "Like I did with my own company."

"Look, Hawthorne, you don't have to—" Lily was the first to object and he shook his head.

"What I'm trying to say is that I'm ready. And I think it's time."

"Oh, it's definitely about time, big bro," Daisy interjected.

"Here's what I've come up with," he flattened his notebook papers in front of him. He walked through the things his father was responsible for on the farm and his thoughts on who would take over each. "Dad still manages all the breeding schedules and kidding for the goats and pigs. I can do that," he looked at the next point.

"I'll do it," Rose spoke up. "I've been trying to get

Dad to give me more control on the livestock side. It's what I went to school for." She lifted her chin. "I've got this, Hawthorne."

Hawthorne raised his eyebrows at his youngest sister's moxie. "Well, alright. Rose has everything livestock related. Just come to me for big purchases and keep me in the loop. Sound good?" Rose nodded and he moved on to the next item. It felt like running a staff meeting, like he had in the old days.

Before long, the roles and responsibilities had been handed out, each of his sisters taking on a little more, or a lot more, based on their input. Hawthorne had more on his plate and he knew there were things he'd forgotten or didn't even realize had been done by his father before. Before they could do anything else, he knew where he needed to go.

"Let's all clean this up and head back into town. Has anyone heard from Mom?" No one had, and as he put the orange juice back into the fridge, Hawthorne saw the neatly packed Thanksgiving leftovers. The fridge was bursting with plastic containers and casserole dishes. It would be like playing Jenga trying to get anything out of this.

"Oh man, I forgot about all the Thanksgiving food. Mom must have been elbow deep in it when Dad had his stroke."

Poppy wiped down the counter and nodded. "The kitchen looked like Daisy's bedroom in middle school—total disaster. It was above and beyond for Avery to stick around and clean it all up so we could go to the hospital."

He'd assumed she left after his family piled into vehicles and followed the ambulance to Terre Haute. Pride swelled within him at Avery's servant heart. It was only more evidence of her thoughtful nature that she would take the time to ensure they could come home to a sanctuary instead of a disaster-zone.

Hawthorne wanted to see her, or at least call her, but he settled for a text message. As of today, he was the Interim General Manager of Bloom's Farm, and there was a lot to do. First, he needed to see his parents.

Lily stuck her head around the corner. "By the way, Mom has no idea you bailed yesterday. She sort of assumed you came back here to take care of things, and none of us had the heart to correct her."

Gratitude flooded him and he nodded. The last thing he'd wanted was to place another worry onto his overwhelmed mother. Hawthorne wasn't proud of how he'd reacted yesterday, but his commitment moving forward was solid. He would tell her the truth later today.

The events of yesterday may have tried to shake his foundation, but the bricks he'd been building with over the last few months proved solid. He knew as long as he continued building upon faith and family, he'd be just fine.

18

*I*n Avery's small apartment living room, she and Hawthorne sat on the floor in front of the coffee table. Half-empty Chinese food containers littered the table in front of them and she had pulled a throw blanket from the couch behind them.

The credits of an old Christmas movie scrolled down the screen in front of them and they laughed at the announcement that the same movie would be starting again. "Twenty-four hours in a row seems a bit excessive," she joked.

Hawthorne winked at her, "Depends on what we're talking about, I'd say." Avery flushed and leaned over to nudge him with her shoulder. Tomorrow they would be at the farm, spending

Christmas day with the entire family. For tonight, she had him all to all herself.

Hawthorne stood up, leaving behind the little cocoon of blankets and pillows she'd constructed for their impromptu take-out picnic, and she gave a pouty look. When he came back, he handed her a small package wrapped in red foil paper. The dramatic forlorn look transformed to a grin and Hawthorne laughed at her.

"I thought we agreed no gifts!" she exclaimed.

He shrugged, "I know. But this is as much for me as it is you." The mysterious comment had tripped her curiosity and Avery quickly unwrapped the checkbook-sized box. It was foolish to be disappointed that it wasn't a ring, but she was.

Inside the small package was an envelope and Avery gave Hawthorne a confused look. When he simply nodded at her to continue, she flipped it open. Inside she found a tourism brochure from Freedom Ridge Resort.

"Umm…. Thank you?" she said. Maybe Hawthorne didn't know her as well as she thought.

Hawthorne smiled, then reached over to open the brochure, revealing a printed trip itinerary. "Spring break," he said.

"We're going to Freedom for Spring Break?"

He nodded and explained, "I'm sure I met your parents fifteen years ago, but I figure it would be good to do it again. You know, now that I'm in love with their daughter."

Avery felt herself blush, like she did every time Hawthorne said he loved her. Sometimes, it still felt like a dream. As though she was still the young girl imagining the handsome brother of her best friend would finally notice her and fall madly in love. Somehow, he really had.

"Plus," Hawthorne continued with a mischievous smile, "I've got a pretty important question I need to ask your father."

Avery felt her mouth fall open and she exhaled a surprised laugh. She set the brochure down and crossed the space between them, propelling herself into his arms and crashing them both to the floor in the tiny space between the couch and coffee table. Hawthorne's laughter rumbled against her and he kissed her temple as he wrapped her in a hug. He pulled them upright and she turned towards him, her heart racing and her breathing rapid and shallow.

Avery met his gaze, basking in the love she saw there. Hawthorne kissed her gently, and she let herself dissolve into the kiss. In his arms, she felt secure. He wasn't perfect, but neither was she. His heart was steady though, and she didn't doubt his commitment to her. When the tender kiss ended, she tucked her head under his chin, hearing his heartbeat beat solidly in her ear.

"I love you, Hawthorne Bloom."

He pulled her hand to his lips and kissed her fingers, "I love you, too."

EPILOGUE

The Christmas tree sparkled in the corner, and the fireplace crackled. There were fewer decorations this year than usual, but the Christmas spirit was alive and well on Bloom's Farm.

Laura smiled at her twins, Daisy and Dandelion, together on the armchair. They'd been practically attached since Andi arrived home a few days ago. She wondered if they even realized how they gravitated to each other. Lavender and Rose sat on the floor, seniority positions on the couch claimed by Poppy and Lily.

Despite the pile of presents under the tree, having all her children home was the only Christmas gift Laura Bloom needed. Her children were home and so was her husband. After one month in a rehabilitation facility after his stroke, Keith was finally released. Speech difficulties and weakened muscles on his left side remained, but, Praise the Lord, her husband was home! She knew it could be so much worse, and she would be forever grateful that his stroke had happened while Hawthorne was there to call for help. The doctors said the quick treatment made a world of difference.

Still, this December was the hardest single month Laura could remember. In true Bloom fashion, Keith tackled the challenges of recovery with vigor. Speech therapy, physical therapy, even children's puzzles frustrated him. But he kept going. Watching the strong, vibrant man she had loved for almost forty years struggle to form a sentence zapped her own strength. Laura often returned from the rehab facility wrung out and exhausted, not sure she could go again tomorrow. But God granted strength to the weary, she was living testament to that.

There were bright spots too, though. Each of her children had been an amazing gift from God this month. Certainly, in an answer to prayers, Hawthorne had grown up in the past few months. Even before Keith's stroke, she saw the redemptive work of Christ in him. And there was Avery, sitting next to him in front of the fire. A satisfied smile on her lips, Laura had to give herself a pat on the back for helping that along. Sometimes, her children just needed a little nudge. What was a mother for, after all?

She had the same feeling about Daisy, who'd just today been complaining about the handsome young contractor Laura had seen around the old house. If she knew her daughter—and Laura was confident she did — it wasn't the man's attitude that bothered Daisy as much as the way he knocked her off kilter. In the very best way.

Hawthorne read the Christmas story from the book of Luke and Laura patted Keith's leg with her hand. Slowly, he reached over with his strong hand to squeeze hers.

"Haa—pp-a?" he stuttered.

She smiled and whispered, "Yes, dear. Incredibly happy."

ABOUT A DATE FOR DAISY

BOOK 1 OF THE BLOOM SISTERS SERIES

*He thinks she's the captain of the Hot Mess Express.
She thinks he's rigid and wound too tight. And this
renovation is about to get complicated.*

Daisy Bloom is determined to turn her 100-year-old
house into a bed and breakfast. The only problem?
She knows nothing about renovations.

Enter Lance Matthews, construction guru and
business owner. He is determined to tackle this
project with his usual methodical, organized
approach. His only problem? The beautiful and
infuriating homeowner -- deeply involved with the
project and completely averse to lists, schedules, or
any form of organization.

When sparks fly between these wildly different

personalities, will they find common ground? Or does God have other plans for each of them?

Will Daisy and Lance overcome their differences? Find out in A Date for Daisy, Book 1 of The Bloom Sisters Series.

NOTE TO READERS

Thank you for picking up (or downloading!) this book. As any author can tell you, reviews are incredibly important to our success. If you enjoyed this book, please take a minute to leave a review.

Hawthorne and Avery were some of my favorite characters yet! And the more I get to know the entire Bloom family, the more excited I am to write each of their stories. Even though this was a short book, Hawthorne and Avery had some real challenges, especially Hawthorne.

I love how Avery helped him recognize and embrace his true purpose. It's easy to lose sight of the person we want to be, especially in the midst of crisis and chaos! It's important to recognize that though

Avery motivated Hawthorne - only God can change someone's heart.

Even when Hawthorne made a mistake, Avery was quick to forgive (as we should be) and encouraged him. Isn't it amazing that we can rest in the knowledge that God will use everything for good - even our mistakes?

I pray daily my books encourage you in your faith and your struggles.

You can learn more about my upcoming projects at my website: www.taragraceericson.com and by signing up for my newsletter, where I share Biblical encouragement, bookish news, and crazy stories from my life. Just for signing up, you will get a free story!

If you've never read my other books, I'd love for you to read the Main Street Minden Series and dive into the world of Minden, Indiana.

Thank you again for all your support and encouragement.

ACKNOWLEDGMENTS

Above all, to my Father in heaven. I am amazed over and over again by your goodness and blessing. My cup runneth over and I praise Your holy name. Keep me close, Father.

To Jessica, I appreciate your friendship so much! I am excited for you as you embark on the business journey of BH Writing Service. As an editor, you are top-notch. As a friend, you are beyond compare.

To Gabbi, for forgiving my flaws and cheering me on. I love you!

To Hannah Jo Abbott and Mandi Blake, my writing circle and sanity keepers. Both of your books are wonderful and I am so glad we have become friends through this crazy writing adventure.

To my mother - the proofreader. I'm so lucky to

have you as a mother. Your support means everything as my life takes twists and turns neither of us ever expected! Thank you for loving me through thick and thin. And for being the first one to buy every book. In multiples.

To my ACFW MOzarks peeps - I love going on this journey with all of you! Keep writing!

Thank you to all my friends and family, named and unnamed here, without whose support and encouragement, I would have given up a long time ago.

And especially, to my husband. It's not always easy to be married to a writer. Your support of this adventure makes this possible. I love you more than words. And to Mr. B and Little C; I cherish every day I spend with you. Mommy loves you!

ABOUT THE AUTHOR

Tara Grace Ericson lives in Missouri with her husband and two sons. She studied engineering and worked as an engineer for many years before embracing her creative side to become a full-time author. Tara says sometimes God asks us to do things the world calls crazy - but that saying "yes" to Him is the most rewarding thing she has ever done.

She loves cooking, crocheting, and reading books by the dozen. Her writing partner is usually her black lab - Ruby - and a good cup of coffee or tea.

She loves a good "happily ever after" with an engaging love story. That's why Tara focuses on writing clean contemporary romance, with an emphasis on Christian faith and living. She wants to encourage her readers with stories of men and women who live out their faith in tough situations.

Made in the USA
Monee, IL
30 July 2022

10551856R00111